CATASTROPHE QUEEN

EMMA HART

NEW YORK TIMES BESTSELLING AUTHOR

ONE

MALLORY

THERE WERE THREE THINGS I NEEDED TO BE WRITTEN ON A T-SHIRT FOR every stranger who passed me in the street.

Red was my nail color.

Dry shampoo was the greatest invention since humans evolved.

I was, without a doubt, the biggest walking disaster since… well, humans evolved.

Of course there were a lot of other things I could say to describe myself. I could eat an abnormal number of tacos in one sitting. I had the gravitational center of a bouncy ball. My tolerance for alcohol was world-record worthy, and if I ever wanted to regain any of the dignity I'd lost thanks to a cracked sidewalk right before senior prom, I'd never wear a heel higher than three inches again.

Even three inches was pushing it.

I much preferred zero.

In fact, I preferred not to wear shoes at all. If I was wearing shoes, there was a better-than-average chance I was leaving the house.

If I was leaving the house, I was socializing.

And let me get this straight right now: I was not a socializer.

You could keep your fancy-schmancy parties and your loud-ass bars and clubs.

I wanted my bunny slippers and my pajama shorts with penguins on.

Yes, I was a closet eighty-year-old, and no, I didn't give a shit what anyone thought about that.

In my not-so-humble and far-too-frequently-expressed opinion, I was a twenty-five-year-old grandma without the burden of grandchildren, and I was totally okay with that.

I mean, I could barely keep myself alive, so there wasn't a chance in hell I'd be able to keep two generations of my offspring living and breathing without some kind of divine intervention.

Don't believe me?

I was living with my parents. And we weren't talking just left college, drowning in student debt, can't live on my own kind of living with my parents.

No, it was three years post flying the nest, lived on my own like a boss living with my parents.

And why was I back at home?

Well, that was a fun story.

See, my apartment building had a fire. The origin of it was currently unknown, and while I'd swear that I wasn't responsible, there may or may not have been a chance that I'd forgotten to turn off my flat iron that morning.

Again, I may have turned it off.

Maybe not.

Regardless, my first-floor apartment had been so badly burned that I'd had no choice but to move back in with my parents.

It wasn't so bad. Not really. They charged me minimal rent so I could save as much as possible to get back on my feet because I'd also been let go from my job, and I didn't have the restrictions teenage-me had.

What did I have?

Well, images of my parents doing things no child should ever witness burned into my retinas.

And we weren't talking walking around in underwear or anything like that. No, we were talking about sex toys on the coffee table, a suspender belt over the back of a dining chair, and actual sex on the sofa.

I wished that were the whole story, but there was, like, ninety percent of that iceberg under the surface, full of memories that I didn't want to pull back up, *thank you very much, Satan.*

Long story short, there was now an alarm on Alexa in every room of the house so they'd know I was ten minutes from home.

Yet, I was still dawdling and walking in the direction of Starbucks instead of my house. I'd just left the only interview I hadn't managed to screw up in the last two weeks, but I still wasn't feeling too hot about my chances.

Probably because I had a pair of dirty underwear in the leg of my pants that I'd discreetly managed to tuck into my sock mid-interview under the guise of an itchy ankle.

That, and I wasn't exactly the most organized person in the world. It wasn't a great situation to be in when you were applying to be a personal assistant, but I figured I could do it, even if it was for the boss of a real estate company.

I hadn't even met the guy. I knew nothing about him except for the fact his name was Cameron Reid, and he ran his family's real estate company. His current full-time personal assistant had decided not to come back from maternity leave, and he didn't like her temporary replacement, so she'd been called in to do interviews.

Meeting Casey Owens probably should have been my

first clue that, no matter how well the interview went, I wasn't a fit at Reid Real Estate. She was tall, slim, and she didn't have a hair out of place.

I was… relatively tall, packed a few extra pounds on my ass, and discovered I'd forgotten the curl the back of my hair five minutes before she called me in.

It reminded me of the time Andie went for her interview in that devil-slash-Prada movie. Or Ugly Betty. All those tall, beautiful, perfect people, and then, there's you.

Or me, in this case.

With my half-uncurled hair and a dirty pair of panties with flamingos on them still tucked into my sock, even as I placed my order at the counter in Starbucks.

It really wasn't any wonder that I was single.

Although, part of that was not my fault, but my ex would tell you differently. I took no responsibility for his issues when it came to getting his soldier to stand to attention. Those were all on him, no matter how many times he tried to claim otherwise.

For all I knew, he'd caught something from one of the women he'd been sleeping with behind my back.

Again: that was also not my fault.

The dirty undies in my sock? My fault. Lying cheat of an ex with a problem getting his cock hard? Not my fault.

Not initially setting the alarm on the Alexa for every day?

Totally my fault.

I took my coffee from the counter and scanned the room for an empty table. There wasn't one, which killed my chances of wasting more time before I went home.

With a sigh, I checked my phone for the time and headed for the door. I was going to end up at home earlier than I'd planned, and I needed to check with my mom to make sure there wasn't anything kinky happening somewhere in the house.

I'd considered bleaching my eyes enough in the last few weeks, thank you.

I was reasonably sure I was safe because my grandfather and great aunt were coming to stay to celebrate Grandpa's eightieth birthday. It was still a miracle my exhibitionist mother shared DNA with either of them. They were ornery and grumpy and fought every ten minutes, but they didn't flash their flesh in the hopes of getting out of a speeding ticket. I wouldn't put it past Aunt Grace, though, on second thought.

Really, it was no wonder I was a walking disaster.

I pulled up my messages and clicked on my mom's name. My thumb was poised to type the burning question of whether or not it was safe to come home when I glanced up.

And saw the car screeching to a stop, mere inches from me.

I screamed and stepped back. My heel caught on the curb, sending me toppling backward, and both my coffee and phone went flying. My cup slammed against the sidewalk, splattering hot liquid everywhere right as I managed to save my phone from certain death by concrete.

My heart was beating so fast it should have exploded, and adrenaline raced through my veins. I gripped my phone against me so tightly that the edges pressed painfully into my skin.

Oh my God.

I'd just almost died.

Maybe slightly dramatic, but I probably wasn't far wrong. I didn't even know I'd stepped into the road. When had that happened? Had I really been in that deep into my own little world that I hadn't even checked for traffic?

Dear God.

How was I still alive?

The back door to the sleek, black car that somehow hadn't run me over swung open. From my vantage position on the sidewalk, the first thing I saw was a pair of shiny, black shoes attached to legs wearing perfectly-pressed, light gray dress pants.

I dragged my gaze up from the feet, over the door of

the perfectly clean car, and stared at the most handsome man known to humankind.

Thick, dark, wavy hair covered his head, curling over his ears. Lashes the same dark shade of brown framed impossibly bright-blue eyes that regarded me with a mixture of shock and concern, and my ovaries about exploded when he rubbed a large hand over full pink lips and a stubbled, strong jaw.

"Miss—I'm so sorry. Are you okay?"

Scrambling to my feet as he approached me, I tugged down the leg of my pants and grabbed my purse. "Yes. I mean—it was my fault. I wasn't paying attention. I'm sorry."

He let go of the car door, showing broad shoulders and just how well that gray suit was tailored to him and picked up my coffee cup. "All the same, I think we can share the blame. Are you sure you're not hurt?"

Just my dignity, and by this point, I was running low on it anyway.

I shifted, taking a step back. "I'm fine, really. Thank you."

"Can I replace your coffee? Give you a ride anyway to apologize?" His expression was so earnest, his concern so genuine that I almost gave in.

Almost.

I had almost walked into the front of his car, then

proceeded to embarrass myself in front of everyone on the street.

"No, no, it's fine. I'm not far from home." I clutched my phone and purse straps a little harder. "Again, thank you, but I should be going."

He nodded as if he understood. "Uh, miss? Did you drop something there?"

My eyes followed the direction Mr. Dreamboat was pointing. On the side of the road, tucked against the curb, was a pair of white, cotton panties with flamingos on them.

My white, cotton panties with flamingos on them.

Swallowing, I met his bright eyes and shook my head. *Dear God, please don't let me blush.* "No. I've never seen them before." I backed up a little more. "Thank you for not running me over."

Mr. Dreamboat grinned, his eyes brightening with his smile. "I'd never be able to forgive myself if I'd been responsible for running over someone as beautiful as you." He glanced toward my panties, then winked at me.

There was no doubting that I was blushing this time around.

You could fry eggs on my cheeks.

So I did the only thing any self-respecting, twenty-five-year-old woman who'd just almost been run over, tripped, and dropped her dirty panties could do.

I ran.

But only like two blocks, because I was in heels, and I had the fitness levels of a hippo.

Then I grabbed a cab.

I was probably safer inside the car.

TENTATIVELY, I PUSHED OPEN THE FRONT DOOR TO THE HOUSE I'D grown up in. I could barely see through the gap into the hall, but I didn't want to look. I wanted to listen.

No creaking. No gasping. No moaning. Only the snuffling and yipping of my mom's Pomeranian, Poochie, as she assaulted a stuffed bear with the danger of a falling leaf.

Thank God the stupid animal was usually asleep in Mom's room. I don't know if I could deal with her running around everywhere all the time. Then again, it wasn't my house, so whatever.

"That's not a dog," came a familiar, old voice. "That's a cotton ball with a squeaker stuffed inside it."

Then my mom's sigh. "Aunt Grace, Poochie is a Pomeranian. She's supposed to be fluffy."

"Poochie is a stupid name for a dog," my great aunt replied. "You know what a poochie is, Helen? It's that pudge you get when you eat too many pies. Not a dog's name, unless you're comparing your dog to your excess stomach fat."

"It's a pleasure to have you here, too," Mom replied dryly.

Well, if Grace was there already insulting my mom, there wasn't a chance I'd stumble onto a weird sex game today.

I pushed the door the rest of the way open and stepped into the hall.

Relief washed across my mom's face, brightening her light-brown eyes. "Mallory! You're back early!"

"No tables at Starbucks," I muttered. "Hello, Aunt Grace. You're looking as lovely as ever."

Aunt Grace narrowed her eyes at me, the ornery old git. "Why are you dirty?"

"Fell over," I replied, dumping my purse at my feet and shrugging out of my blazer to hang it up. "Why does your dress look like a kindergarten class threw up their paints on it?"

"Because I stopped giving a shit about what other people thought of me fifty years ago." She gave me a toothy grin, her eyes sparkling. "Did you know you have a giant rip on your ass?"

Wait—what?

I clapped my hands on my butt cheeks and, sure as hell,

there was a tear on my right ass cheek. Not 'giant' as she'd claimed, but big enough that anyone looking could see I was wearing not-very-big-panties.

What? These pants hugged my ass, and nobody liked panty lines.

At least, these pants did. All they'd be hugging now was the inside of a trash can.

"Shit." I smoothed my hands. "And I liked these pants."

"Bet my dress looks pretty good now, huh?" Aunt Grace's eyes lit up.

Poochie eyed her for a second before she returned to her soft toy.

"Where's Grandpa? Did you fly in together?" I untucked the plain white tee I'd worn under the blazer and tugged it down over my ass to cover the rip for now.

"At the liquor store," Mom said with an edge to her voice, turning to go to the kitchen. "The first thing he did when he got here was check the liquor cabinet to see if we had, to quote him, "the good stuff.""

Aunt Grace leaned in. "Jack Daniels. His best buddy."

"But we have Jack," I replied, following my elderly aunt to the kitchen. "You bought some last week."

"Yes," Mom replied, turning off the coffee machine. "I bought that for me. Do you think I can get through the next week sober? Between Aunt Grace criticizing everything from my highlights to my dog and Dad asking when you're going to get your life together, I need something for my nerves."

And sex on the dining table wasn't going to be possible. How very woe-is-me of her.

"My life is totally together," I retorted. "All right, so I live here, and I'm trying to get a job, but it could be worse."

Aunt Grace slid onto a stool at the island, wincing as she got comfortable. "Yeah, Mallory. You could have a rip on your ass."

I blinked at my great aunt, taking in her rose-gold-streaked, gray hair that was curled and coiffed to perfection around her wrinkled, powdered face. Her eyes were identical to my mom's, a light golden-brown color that sometimes glinted amber if the light caught them right.

Her thin lips were caked in bright pink lipstick that smudged at the corners of her mouth, and those corners were currently tugged up in a self-satisfied smile.

I crossed to the cabinet where my mom kept the hard liquor and reached inside for the red-capped bottle of Smirnoff vodka and pulled it out. Standing, I tucked the bottle into the crook of my elbow and looked at my relatives.

Mom smirked. "What are you doing with that?"

I looked her in the eye and said, "Doing the same thing you did with your buddy Jack. Hiding it to get me through the week.'"

Her laughter mingled with my great aunt's as I stomped to the stairs, still cradling the bottle. I made a tiny detour to grab my purse and made my way upstairs to the only sacred space I had left: my bedroom.

It was the only place in the house that I could confirm my parents hadn't had sex in, and that was because I'd put a lock on the door when I was eighteen, and I had the only key.

In hindsight, eighteen-year-old me was way smarter than me now.

Then again, me now was hiding a liter bottle of vodka in my bedroom, so who was really winning here?

I kicked the door shut behind me and set the bottle on top of my dresser. There was no doubt in my mind I'd need that vodka by the time the night was through, and that didn't even count this afternoon's antics by me.

I pulled my tee over my head and undid the button on my pants. I was sad about them. They made my ass look at least ten percent peachier and perkier than it actually was, and that was something I could get on board with.

In fact, I believed that all pants should have that perk.

Denim companies would make a mint, especially around the holidays. Spanx were killing it on the stomach thing, after all, but they'd never quite cut it on my ass.

That was probably the fault of my ass, to be honest.

I switched the smart interview outfit for yoga pants and a tank top that stated that I drank well with others and went back downstairs, phone in hand. I wasn't letting go of the damn thing until I found out if I'd gotten the job today or not.

"What's for dinner?" I asked, joining my mom and aunt in the kitchen.

"Lasagna," Mom replied, holding a pasta sheet in the air.

Aunt Grace turned her head to look at me, the pasta sheet box in her hands, and narrowed her eyes at me. "Why are you holding your phone so tightly? Is it an extra appendage you've had attached to yourself?"

I rolled my eyes and sat down at the island. "No. I had a job interview today, and she never said when she'd let me know, so just in case…"

"You're going to be more attached to it than your cousin James was to his penis when he was a teenager?"

"I'm sorry to disappoint you, Aunt Grace, but I have no knowledge of James and his penis," I said simply. "But yes, I'm going to be attached. I don't want to miss the call either way."

She nodded, handing Mom a couple more sheets of pasta. "It's about time you got a job. Or married."

I choked on my own spit. "About time I got a job? I've been out of work for a month, and that was because the company shut down! It's hardly my fault."

"I stitched t-shirts when I was your age and I needed money."

"Yes, but we don't live in the eighteen-hundreds anymore."

Aunt Grace narrowed her eyes even more and wiggled one finger at me. "Your attitude stinks. That's why you're single, jobless, and living with your parents."

Mom froze.

"Is that why you haven't died yet? God isn't ready for your shit and wants to inflict pain on our innocent souls for a little longer?" I shot back.

Slowly, Mom turned around and looked at me, eyes wide.

Silence tightened the air in the kitchen, and I stared down Aunt Grace for a good, long minute.

Until her eyes crinkled, her lips curved into a grin, and her wrinkled cheeks flushed with her laughter. "Atta girl. Maybe that's why you're single. You're too much of a smartass."

"Coming from you, I'll take that as a compliment."

Mom pinched the bridge of her nose and shook her head. "Why did I agree to this again?"

"Because you've got three bottles of Jack in your closet and a Pepsi under the bed." I quirked a brow.

"Aunt Grace is right. You are a smartass."

"It's genetic," I quipped.

"Of course it is." Aunt Grace put the pasta back in the cupboard. "It's the only way to deal with the insufferable men in this family. Be such an obnoxious smartass they go to another room and leave you the hell alone."

Now there was a quote for a cross-stitch.

TWO

MALLORY

TWO HOURS LATER, MY DAD AND GRANDPA HAD RETURNED FROM THE liquor store—and the bar, not that they admitted as much—and my phone was still call-free.

I was okay with it. Mostly because my can of Pepsi wasn't just Pepsi, just like my mom's wasn't.

There were two ways to get through any family gathering: alcohol or a one-way ticket to Cuba.

Since I was short on funds, alcohol it was.

I mean, there was a reason I was such a disaster of a human being. Aside from my parents having a cringey sex life that I knew far too much about, the older generation of the Harper family was an even bigger mess.

Great Aunt Grace was an ex-acrobat who'd turned to chain-smoking and drinking whiskey from the bottle after divorcing her fourth husband. She had a sharp tongue and penchant for criticizing everything except movies with a shirtless Channing Tatum.

Last year, for her seventieth birthday, she'd demanded a trip to Vegas to watch Magic Mike Live, and out of the ten of us who'd gone, she'd enjoyed it the most.

She'd even thrown her underwear at them. It was a sight nobody ever needed to see.

As for Grandpa Eddie—well, he was special. Just a few days shy of eighty, he'd maintained all his mental faculties and had a wit sharper than a knife, and he was one of the only people who could hold a candle to Aunt Grace and make her shut up in the process. Partial to a glass of scotch on birthdays and champagne on Christmas and wine every other night of the year, he smoked big, fat, Cuban cigars and wasn't afraid to tell you to get the hell out of his personal space.

Honestly, if I could grow up to be a combination of them in sixty years, I'd be more than happy.

I'd be old, grumpy, and just this side of being an alcoholic.

Would I get to wave my stick at people and tell them to get off my lawn, too? That was probably the only way their existence could get any better. Although, given my luck, there was every chance I'd trip over my own feet and knock myself out with the walking stick.

Clearly, I hadn't been blessed with Aunt Grace's ability to balance on, well, a flat sidewalk, as evidenced by the graze on my right butt cheek.

I couldn't cross a road, never mind perform stunts on a tightrope.

"I'm telling you, Helen, it wasn't my fault his chicken ran in front.of my car!" Grandpa took a long drag on his cigar and puffed it out in little circles. "The damn creatures have a life of their own! Who keeps chickens in the city? We don't live in bumfuck country land."

Mom took a deep breath and slowly let it out.

"There's a brake for a reason, you fool," Aunt Grace snapped at him. "Use it!"

"I do use it. Just not when flying, feathered, little shit-droppers are in front of my car." He sniffed and leaned back in the armchair. "They got wings. They can use 'em."

Aunt Grace rolled her eyes, simultaneously reaching for her whiskey and a cigarette. "They might have wings, but their brains are smaller than their shit droppings. They ain't gonna move."

"Is there a reason we're discussing chicken poop?" I asked, looking around.

"Is there a reason you've got vodka in that can of Pepsi?" Grandpa shot back at me.

Narrowing my eyes, I met his amused gaze. "Yes. So the act of listening to you complain about chicken shit isn't quite as painful."

"Better the chicken shit than Grace's obsession with that male stripper movie."

Aunt Grace visibly shuddered.

Dad's eyes widened. "Why don't we talk about something a little less...dividing? Mallory, honey, how did your job interview go today?"

Everyone's eyes looked my way. Like Mom and Aunt Grace didn't already know.

I shifted on the sofa. Man, I should not have been so conservative with the vodka in this can. "It went well. Better than a lot of others lately, so there's that. I think I might have a chance."

"Did you tell them you'd once confused February with September?" Grandpa chuckled.

"I did not," I replied. "I simply forgot that February only had twenty-eight days. It's a common mistake."

Aunt Grace leaned forward, silver smoke curling upward from her cigarette. "How about the time you thought it was Friday and went to school when it was Saturday?"

"All right, enough." I grabbed my Pepsi can and finished the rest of it before jumping up off the sofa. "I could absolutely be someone's personal assistant, and that's that."

"How?" Aunt Grace continued. "You're a night owl,

you don't like other people, and you have the organizational skills of a two-year-old in a toy box."

"And you're seventy with an unhealthy obsession with a movie star half your age, should probably have stock in Marlboro cigarettes, and you've got a bit of a drinking problem, but you don't hear me shouting that from the rooftops." I tipped my can in her direction and left the room to the sound of Grandpa laughing so hard he wheezed.

I grabbed the wine from the fridge and pulled a glass down from the cupboard. Not only could I not be bothered to go upstairs to get the vodka, I wasn't in the mood to get anything watered down.

This situation would have been fine if I'd had an apartment to go to.

Unfortunately, all I had a was a bedroom and an aunt who wouldn't stop bugging me if I fucked off upstairs and hid for the rest of the night.

"Mal?" Mom yelled. "Your phone is ringing?"

I almost dropped the bottle of wine onto the counter, only just a breath away from knocking over my wine glass. I took a deep breath and stopped to right them both before running into the living room and diving to the coffee table for my phone.

"Hello?" I breathed into it.

It rang again.

"Shit!" I scrambled to press the green button on the screen and tried again. "Hello?"

"Are the crazies in town yet?" came the familiar tones of my best friend, Jade, into my ear.

"Is it the job?" Mom stage-whispered.

"No, it's Jade." I sighed.

"Happy to talk to you, too, asshole," Jade sniped in my ear.

"Hold on," I said, standing up straight. "Gimme a minute."

"If that's how you answer a phone at work," Aunt Grace said, "Make sure you don't have a rip in your pants."

I flipped her the bird and, after detouring to the kitchen, took the stairs. "What's up?" I asked Jade.

Laughter tinkled through the line. "Well, I was asking if the crazies are here, but I'd know Grace's voice miles away."

I groaned, sitting on my bed and cradling my stemless glass. "She's been on my back more than a hooker is on her own," I replied. "She's trying to be funny, but all she's doing is bringing out my inner asshole."

"Your inner asshole? You mean you keep some locked away?"

"Don't try me, Jade Lincoln. I will kill you in your sleep."

"No, you won't. You couldn't function without me.

How'd the interview go?"

Unlike my family, I told her absolutely everything from the moment I walked through the door to the moment I finally escaped my family in the kitchen and got to take off my ripped pants.

"Are we talking Jamie Dornan working out in Fifty Shades hot or Hemsworth brother hot?"

"Both. Combined." I reached for the glass on the nightstand and sipped. "I've never been so embarrassed in my life. Of all my underwear, it had to be the flamingo pair."

"I've warned you about those," Jade laughed down the line. "I said one day they'd come back to haunt you."

"But they were so cute!"

"You didn't pick them up?"

"No!" My voice went so high I was I was only an octave or two from only being audible to dogs. "How could I pick them up? I told him they weren't mine! I couldn't admit to dropping my panties in the gutter! That wouldn't make a good story for the grandkids."

"For the—Jesus, Mal. You dropped your underwear from your pants leg, in public, right after you'd almost walked in front of an extremely hot guy's car. The only thing you're gonna be telling your grandkids is how much of a klutz you were in your twenties."

"And my teens, and my pre-teens, and—"

"Every day since you learned to walk," Jade finished.

"You should have picked up the panties. You loved those."

"You literally just reminded me about how you warned me about them."

"I know, but for my own amusement, you should have picked them up."

"I wasn't thinking about your amusement, you bitch. I was thinking that I'd never been so mortified in my entire life."

"I don't know," she said slowly. "We can probably come up with a shortlist."

I groaned again and sank back into my pillow, resting my wine on my stomach. "I quit. I give up. I'm too much of a mess for this world."

"Oh, quit being so fucking dramatic. You're just fine. You're never going to see that guy again, and if you do, he probably won't even recognize you."

She might have been going for comforting, but all she was doing was bruising my ego a little bit.

"You're probably right," I sighed. "Still, the dream was nice while it lasted. Better than the crap happening downstairs, at least."

"Grandpa Eddie still angry at the neighbor's chickens?"

"Like you wouldn't believe. He thinks they're out to get him. I think he's going to do something drastic like, I don't know, start throwing lit matches or something."

She laughed. "Well, on the bright side, the matches

would probably go out before they even hit the chickens."

"Do you think they'd go out if I threw some at Grandpa?"

"He drinks so much he'd just go up in flames from being in the same room as the flames. How the hell is he eighty?"

"When I figure it out, I'll let you know. We could bottle that shit and sell it."

"No kidding." She paused right as the sound of Aunt Grace screaming about someone being a cheater broke through the air. "Oh no. Did they—"

"Bring out Trivial Pursuit?" I sighed. "Sounds like it. Gotta go. I'll call you if I hear anything from that job."

"All right. I have bail money if you need it. Ciao."

The chance that I would was pretty great.

MY EARS WERE RINGING.

It was really irritating. And it wouldn't stop. Over and over and—

Oh, shit. That wasn't my ears. That was my phone!

Rolling over with my eyes still closed, I threw my arm out to the nightstand and swatted at the surface for my phone. My pinky finger barely connected with it, yet a dull thud told me I'd sent the phone flying straight to the floor.

It stopped ringing.

"No, no, no!" I opened my eyes and flung myself over the side of the bed, just missing the corner of the nightstand with my forehead, and grabbed the phone.

It still worked.

Thank God. I'd only missed the call.

It was an unknown number, but one that was familiar to me. I stared at the screen for a moment with sleep in my eyes until a text popped up that I had a voicemail.

Immediately, I called, rubbing my eyes to wake up a little, and hit the button to listen to a new message.

"Hello, this is Casey Owens from Reid Real Estate. I'm calling for Mallory Harper regarding our interview for the personal assistant position yesterday. I'll be in the office until twelve-thirty. You can reach me at…" She trailed off, reciting the number, and I scrambled out of bed to grab a pen and paper from the desk under my window.

I'd missed it, so I listened again and jotted down the number before calling back. It was picked up after three rings.

"Good morning, you've reached Cameron Reid's office. Casey speaking. How may I help you?"

"Hi, Ms. Owens?" Great, my voice cracked. I cleared my throat. "This is Mallory Harper returning your message."

"Oh, Mallory, hi!" Her voice brightened. "Did I catch you at a bad time?"

"Not at all—sorry, we have family over, and I just missed your call. What can I do for you?"

"Actually, I was calling to tell you that I was very impressed with your interview yesterday."

Well, thank God someone was.

"If you're still available, I'd like to offer you the position. Pending a trial period, of course."

Holy shit.

"Wow. Thank you so much—of course. I'd love it."

Woohoo! Finally!

"Great! Can you come in tomorrow morning so we can get started on your training? Say, eight-thirty?"

"Oh, of course. That's not a problem."

"Brilliant. I'll see you then, Mallory, and congratulations!"

"Thank you," I said, dazed. "Goodbye."

I hung up and dropped my phone.

Holy shit. I got the job. I actually got the freaking job.

Yanking open my door, I almost tripped over the rug in the hall as I made my way to the stairs. "Mom! Dad! I got it! I got the job!" My footsteps thundered against the stairs as I ran down and into the kitchen. "I got the job!"

Aunt Grace looked up from her paper. "But you didn't get any pants on."

I glanced down. She was right. I was in a tank top and panties. Damn it. "But I got the job!"

"What job?" Grandpa groused from behind me. "Are you a hooker?" He shuffled past me into the kitchen. "Where's my breakfast?"

Mom rolled her eyes and hugged me. "Well done, sweetie. Go put some pants on and then you can tell us all about it."

The urge to make a snarky comment about the irony of her telling someone else to put their pants on, but I was on too much of a high to do that. Or even care that I had my ass out, to be honest. As long as I remembered to put them on the next day, I was good.

"Mallory. Put your pants on. Don't be like your mother," Aunt Grace snapped, giving the snark for me.

"Aunt Grace!" Mom gasped.

"She ain't wrong, Helen." Grandpa looked around the kitchen. "Where are the pancakes?"

Mom gritted her teeth. "I didn't make them yet. Oliver had to run to the store for milk, and he isn't back."

Grandpa muttered something under his breath and popped out his teeth. At the table.

"Eddie! Nobody wants to see those gnashers! They're bad enough in your mouth when you smile like a serial killer!" Aunt Grace shouted, reaching over with the straw from Mom's glass of water and prodding the dentures with it.

Mom gasped.

That was my cue to leave.

Granted, my cue probably should have been when Aunt Grace told me I had no pants on, but whatever.

The front door opened right as I stepped onto the bottom stair. It was Dad, returning from the store with a brown bag tucked against his body.

"Run. Save yourself," I hissed at him. "It's a mess in there."

He looked at my legs. "Are you aware you aren't wearing pants?"

"More aware than you normally are," I retorted, grinning. "By the way, I got the job."

His face lit up. "Great. How long until you move out?"

"Around the same time you start listening to the alarm I set you." I blew him a kiss and ran up the stairs.

It was going to be a long, long day.

THREE

MALLORY

THE BUILDING THAT HOUSED REID REAL ESTATE WASN'T INTIMIDATING by any means. No, like much of the downtown area in Dansville, Colorado, where I'd grown up, it straddled the line between the affluent neighborhood and the regular area.

I didn't want to say poor. It wasn't poor. Working class? I wasn't sure, but it wasn't mansions like the other side of town was, that was for sure.

Anyway. Reid Real Estate was a simple, three-story building that had once been home to the town's founder. It'd apparently been snapped up in an auction in the early nineteen-hundreds by Cameron Reid's great-great-grandfather so his son could open his own business buying and selling houses, and aside from a couple of name changes to keep up with the times, nothing about it had changed.

The exposed brick façade meant it blended in with the rest of Main Street, especially the buildings at the more luxurious end of the street, but the pristine, white sign with stocky black lettering made it stand out.

I'd pulled out my best clothes for today—a fitted black dress with a high collar and sleeves that cut off at the shoulders. I'd partnered it with a cream blazer and shiny, black flats.

I didn't need any encouragement to fall over today.

Nerves rolled in my stomach as I approached the building. I wanted—no—I needed this job. I needed to get back my independence, and the salary for this job would mean I'd have a down payment for a rental apartment within a few months. I'd probably have to use some patio furniture for a while, but we all had to make sacrifices.

I needed not to screw this up. It was a tall order, really, considering that screwing things up was what I did best.

No.

I couldn't think like that.

I had to go into this building like I owned it, and that was exactly what I was going to do.

I opened the front door and stepped in. Unfortunately for me, there was a tiny step, around three inches in height, that I'd completely missed. I stumbled but quickly managed to right myself thanks to my flat shoes and a death grip on the door handle.

My cheeks burned as I looked up and around to make sure nobody had seen me.

I wasn't so lucky.

Casey stood at the bottom of the staircase that lead to the top floor where Cameron Reid's office was. She grinned.

"Well, this is off to an excellent start," I said, letting go of the door.

Casey laughed, pushing a wisp of blonde hair from her face. "Don't worry. You'd be surprised how many people do that. At least you're wearing flats. The last girl we trailed had gone out to get coffee in four-inch-heels and missed the step." She winked.

"Yeah. If you knew me, you wouldn't be surprised if I said I'll probably do that at some point. Without the heels, though. Flats are clearly dangerous enough."

She laughed again, holding her hand out for me to shake. "It's great to see you again, Mallory. The other agents mostly keep their own hours, but we have a couple of new hires who'll show up around nine to get a head start on their portfolio. I'll give you a quick tour before we head upstairs."

And it was a quick tour. There wasn't a lot to show, really. The main area where the front door was housed two desks and a receptionist's desk that Casey explained belonged to the new agents and the secretary who ran everyone else's business. The stairs in the hallway were surrounded by three rooms—a restroom, a small kitchen, and one private office for one of the more successful agents.

Upstairs was much the same. The hallway was set out as a waiting area with two cream, leather sofas, bushy green plants, and magazines scattered. It'd been renovated to provide three offices, one of which was currently empty. Apparently, Reid Real Estate was picky about who they hired full-time, and only one of the new hires would get a permanent place here.

Then, Casey waved me up a second flight to stairs to the top floor. It was more spacious than the others, mostly because two rooms had been knocked through to make one large office for Cameron Reid. Like downstairs, there was a small waiting area with another two spotless cream sofas just a few feet away from what was, now, my desk.

"Let me finish showing you here, and then we'll get stuck into the desk." Casey lead me over to a swinging door that lead to a smaller hallway with two doors. "Down here is Mr. Reid's private bathroom and kitchen. They are for the use of him and yourself only. The only exception made to this bathroom is pregnant ladies." She winked. "Otherwise, this area is off limits to both employees and clients."

"Why can I use it then?"

"Do you want to carry coffee up two flights of stairs?"

"I can't think of a worse idea, actually." Knowing my luck, it'd be more like six by the time I was done spilling it.

Casey smiled. "Now, the bathroom." She opened the door to a large, white bathroom with turquoise accents. There was a walk-in shower in the corner, plus a sink, mirror, and toilet. "The cleaners come every night at seven, but it's your job to ensure they've done theirs correctly. All you have to do is check the towels are clean and that there is adequate toilet paper."

"Sounds easy enough," I replied. "What about the kitchen?"

"Again, the cleaning staff will take care of it." She held the door open for me. "It's nothing fancy, but this is your responsibility. You have to make sure the coffee beans are always stocked, that the milk is fresh, and that you always buy the right sweetener."

"Sweetener?"

"Yep. Mr. Reid's grandmother came and gave him a public lecture about his overuse of three sugars in every coffee, so he switched. But…" She took a few steps back and opened a cupboard. "If he's having a bad day, slip a couple sugars in instead for your own sanity."

"You make him sound like a monster."

She laughed, shutting the cupboard. "God, no. He's been a delight to work for, but I'd rather be at home with my baby girl." She shrugged. "You'll get along just fine.

Now, he typically brings his lunch with him, but on occasion, he'll ask you to go out and get some. This doesn't cut into your break at all, but you do have to make sure all his calls go through Amanda at the main reception. She'll take messages and give them to you on your way back in to return calls."

"Okay."

"You get forty-five minutes for lunch every day, plus one fifteen-minute break in the afternoon. I would advise going out for lunch, or you'll get roped into doing something, but take your break in the kitchen." She ushered me out of the room and back into the hall area. "Overwhelmed yet?"

"A little," I admitted, putting my purse on the floor next to my desk.

Casey smiled sympathetically. "Don't worry. All this is written down for you, but I'm only here until after you get back from lunch, then I have to get my daughter, so I want to get through it."

"Okay. I've got this. It's fine."

It was not fine. How many sugars did my boss take again?

Wait, no. It wasn't even sugar. It was sweetener. Jesus.

"Take a seat." Casey wheeled the chair out for me.

I sat.

"The first thing you need to know is that the desk is set

up to my organizational system. Please keep it that way just in case you don't make it past the trial, but I'm fairly confident you will." She then proceeded to show me where everything was in the desk, from paperclips to staplers to important files. "The cabinets behind you are home to current information on available listings. The cabinet on the right…" She walked over and opened each drawer. "Top drawer: houses for sale. Middle drawer: houses for let. Third drawer: land for sale. They are marked in case you forget."

"Sale, let, land. Got it."

"The second unit is for commercial properties. We don't have a lot—maybe two right now. Don't worry about this one so much." She shot me a dazzling smile and hit a button on the side of the computer screen.

It blinked to life.

"Here's your login. It's only temporary right now, but if you get the job permanently, I'll be here to make sure you're settled and change it all up for you. Pop it in the box there." She tapped one blue fingernail against the screen.

I typed, conscious of my chipping red nails. I really needed to paint them. In my lunch hour, damn it.

I logged in and froze. There were icons everywhere.

"Ugh. Excuse me." Casey leaned forward. "This should have been sorted. I asked one of the new hires to organize all these files for you."

A few clicks later and the screen was much more

tolerable to look at, and a hell of a lot less confusing.

"Okay. Let's start simple, and I'll explain those to you. Phone." She pointed at the wireless phone on a dock to my right. "Simple. If it rings, someone wants you or they want Mr. Reid."

"Do I have to send a call through to him?"

"Sometimes. There is a list of people who go through to him if he's here and not in a meeting or out with a client." She slid it toward me. "It's limited to his parents, his sister, and a few high-profile clients. But, you always put them on hold and call to see if he's able to take the call."

"Okay. Answer, and if they're on the list, put them on hold, check with him, and put them through."

"Yep." She rounded the desk and showed me how to do it, and it was much easier than I thought it would be. "So, the computer..."

The next ten minutes consisted of Casey logging me into all the programs I needed and showing me where the files were. As well as organizing meetings and viewings and phone calls, it was also my job to send information to prospective clients. If they were looking at a specific property or types of property, I had to gather and provide all the information for them.

And, as Casey said, we always said: "by the end of the day."

It'd been thirty minutes, and I was already

overwhelmed. There was so much to take in—so much info that I didn't think I'd remembered a damn thing.

"Okay." Casey clapped her hands and bounced. "I'm going to stand by the window and call you and see how you do. Remember, let it ring two times before you answer."

"Um, okay." I had a lump in my throat the size of a small planet.

The phone rang. I let it ring two times and picked up. "Good morning, this is Cameron Reid's office. Mallory speaking. How can I help you?"

"Oh, good morning. I'm looking for a three-bed, two-bath property in the area. Do you have anything available?"

My eyes widened.

Panic.

Did we? I didn't know.

Casey smiled and held the phone to her chest. "Think. You don't know off the top of your head. What do you need to do?"

I took a deep breath. "Ask if they're renting or buying, confirm that we do, and take an email address to send information over, or arrange an appointment to come in and talk to Mr. Reid."

She pointed a finger at me to continue.

"Do you have anything available?" Casey continued.

"Yes, ma'am. Are you looking to rent or buy?"

"To buy."

"We do have a number of properties available for you to look at. Would you like me to email you some information on them, or would you prefer to come in and take a look yourself?"

Casey grinned. "Email would be great. Here, it's blah blah blah," she finished. "Will it take long?"

"I'll have it to you by the end of the day."

"Perfect, thank you so much." Casey hung up. "There, you would thank them for calling Reid Real Estate and reiterate that you'll be in touch. Good job, Mallory. I know it's tough, but you'll have the hang of it in a week."

"Let's hope so," I muttered. "I feel like I'm drowning."

"No, you'll be fine. My number is in the book in the drawer, and my email is already in your contacts list. If you need anything, Amanda is there to help and so am I until you settle in. I promise this is an easy job. There are no surprises whatsoever."

Heavy footsteps echoed on the stairs.

Casey brightened. "Oh, good. Mr. Reid is here early today. I was hoping to be able to introduce you."

My hands shook under the desk. Oh, God, why was I shaking? That wasn't going to make a good impression whatsoever.

"No, I can't do today. Because I said so," the voice said. It was vaguely familiar.

"Mother, no. I'm busy all day." The man the voice

belonged to stepped into the room.

My stomach sunk.

Thick, wavy, dark hair that curled over his ears.

Bright-blue eyes.

A strong jaw dotted with dark stubble.

A light-gray suit that hugged his body better than any fabric had a right to.

It was Mr. Dreamboat.

Oh, no.

Casey opened her mouth, but he held up a finger, his jacket draped over his forearm as he carried a sleek leather briefcase in his hand. His eyes darted toward us for barely a second, something flickering in them when they landed on me.

I swallowed as his office door swung shut behind him.

Casey eyed me speculatively. "Do you know him?"

"Um." I swung my gaze from his door to her. "Not really. We've had a…fleeting meeting."

"Please don't tell me you've slept with him."

"No! Oh God, no. Nothing like that." My cheeks flushed.

"Oh, thank God." She pressed her hand to her chest and leaned on the desk. "What is it, then?"

I bit my lip and dragged it between my teeth. "After I left the interview, I grabbed Starbucks, and I was kind of in my own little world. I might have stepped into the road without checking it, and I might have fallen over in front of his car trying not to get run over."

Casey's eyes widened. "Oh. *Oh.* You're the crazy girl he was muttering about yesterday morning."

I dropped my head to the desk, the keyboard slamming as I wrote God only knew what on the screen with my forehead.

"Well, if nothing else, this will be interesting."

The amusement in her voice told me she was looking forward to this meeting.

I was glad someone was.

FOUR

CAMERON

"YES, MOM, GOODBYE." I FINALLY HUNG UP AND SET MY PHONE screen-down on my desk.

I loved the woman, but fuck me dead, she forgot I was a grown man running her business and no longer needed her to do my laundry.

I rubbed my hands down my face and blew out a long breath. I had a day full of meetings and a house viewing with one of my most difficult clients ever. I didn't need my mother on my back about...

Shit. I had no idea what she'd even wanted. That's how much I'd been listening. I was going to get it in the neck anyway, so at least now she had a reason.

On top of all that, my new assistant was starting today. Thanks to my mother I was sure I hadn't put on a great first impression. There was no doubt in my mind that my hand up and quick glance had been nothing but rude.

Not that Casey would care. I didn't care about what she thought. She was my cousin, for chrissakes. But the new girl?

The one who'd been sitting behind the desk?

She was familiar to me. Oddly so. I hadn't gotten a long enough look at her to be able to place her, but I knew I'd seen her before. Recently, too.

Who the hell was she?

I dropped my hands and looked at my desk. There was a stack of paper draped over my keyboard, and the first sheet had a bright yellow Post-It note slapped in the middle of the page.

Pulling them toward me, I tugged at the yellow square and read Casey's immaculate, script handwriting.

Mallory Harper – your new assistant. Read this and pretend you care.

I grunted and balled the note up. Whatever. She wasn't going to last long—for whatever reason, nobody did. I'd had three assistants since Casey had gone on maternity leave six months earlier.

I was about ready to steal Amanda from downstairs and find a new receptionist for the other realtors.

Still, I sighed and picked up the resume she'd left for me to read. I scanned it. She was twenty-five and had recently lost her job when her previous company folded. She had lots of experience as an admin assistant, some waitressing, and one short stint in a call center. Lots of casual jobs, but no real direction, despite having a degree in business.

The only good thing here was the admin assistant experience and the fact that, excluding the call center job, she'd lasted a long time in each of her jobs.

Waitressing had gotten her through college—which was also when she'd had her call center job—and she'd been an admin assistant ever since she'd graduated.

She had potential.

She was still familiar to me.

I put the paper down and stared at the wall. It was times like this I wish I'd put a glass panel in. Surely, if I stared at her long enough, I'd figure it out, wouldn't I?

Not that staring at your newest employee was the way to go. Despite my recent track record with personal assistants, I did actually like to keep my employees.

Except for the last one. Answering the phone, still drunk, at ten in the morning, wasn't the image I was hoping to portray with my family's company.

A knock rattled my door, and I took a deep breath as I said, "Come in."

The door creaked open to reveal Casey holding a steaming mug of coffee. "I made coffee," she said unnecessarily, raising the cup like an offering to a deity.

"Thanks." I waved her in. "How's the new girl doing?"

Casey clicked the door shut behind her. "Her name is Mallory. Didn't you read the sheet?"

"No, I used it to wipe my arse this morning."

She clicked her tongue. "You're such a child."

"Then stop acting like my big sister." I grinned, taking the coffee from her.

"You'd be a nicer person if you had one, so the job is left to me." She rolled her eyes and tucked her skirt under her thighs and sat down. "She's doing good. I think she's a little overwhelmed, but I have to get Tilly at twelve-thirty, so I don't have a lot of time to train her. Will you be gentle with her this afternoon?"

I sighed. "I wish I could. I'm not here all afternoon. I have two meetings before lunch, then immediately after, the Carlisles have two viewings for beach houses on the coast. It's an hour each way, so she'll be gone by the time I leave."

Casey winced. "Damn it. She needs someone here who knows what they're doing."

"Move Ellen into the office temporarily and reroute her phone line downstairs. Amanda can help her."

She raised her eyebrows. "Ellen? You want to move her?"

"Why not? She's doing a better job than Sydney right now. Besides, it's only for one day."

"She's going to be running up and down the stairs all afternoon, Cam. You can't put her through that."

I threw out my hands. "What do you want me to do, Case? You know my schedule. I have a viewing tomorrow first thing, and then I'm here all day. You could have had her start tomorrow."

She wiggled her finger at me, her nail blurring blue through the air. "May I remind you, cuz, that I'm doing you a favor? I should be at home with my baby, not pumping my boobs in the bathroom while you flit your way through assistants like they're toilet paper."

All right, that was an exaggeration.

"First, I don't want to know what you do with your boobs, feeding Tilly or otherwise," I said. "Second, I know what you're doing, and I appreciate it. Do you want me to cancel the Carlisles and put them off until tomorrow?"

Slumping in the chair, she ran her hand over her sleek ponytail. "No, I can't do that. Look—she'll be fine. It might help that you aren't here. She won't have to worry about whether you need sugar instead of sweetener or dealing with any of your up-their-ass clients."

"Are you sure?"

"Have I run your life for five years or not?"

"My professional life," I said slowly.

Her eyes narrowed. "And if you'd let me get in there with your personal one, you'd never have dated that gold digger."

"Cynthia wasn't a gold digger. She just had expensive taste."

"If that makes you feel better, you keep telling yourself that." She rolled her eyes. "Mallory will be fine. She's smart. She's got this, but I do have to introduce you to her before you leave."

I pinched the bridge of my nose. "I know her from somewhere, Case. She looks familiar."

"Did you sleep with her?"

"No. I'm a virgin."

"Yeah, me too. Tilly is actually Jesus, born by immaculate conception," she drawled, sarcasm tilting every syllable. "Did you?"

I shook my head and looked over her head toward the wall where my new assistant was sitting—behind a few inches of brick, that was. "No. I haven't slept with her. I'd have remembered her name if I did."

"You're a regular Romeo."

"Shut up. Can you find out a little more about her? I don't have time to get to know her today."

Casey grinned. Slowly, she leaned forward on my desk on her elbows, touching her fingertips together in an evil genius pose. "I already know how you know her."

I quirked an eyebrow. "You do?"

"Yup."

A phone rang from outside my office.

My cousin stood up, a total shit-eating grin on her face, and headed for the doorway. "Sorry, I need to make sure your new assistant is doing okay on the phone."

"Casey—"

The door slammed behind her before I tell her to get her stupid ass back in here.

Ugh.

I needed to talk to my aunt about her daughter's attitude.

It wasn't working for me now that she wasn't.

And who the fuck was Mallory Harper?

I'D BARELY STEPPED OUT OF MY CAR WHEN MY PHONE RANG. ANTONIA Wellington's name flashed on the screen, and I had half a mind to let it run to voicemail and pretend I was driving.

Unfortunately for me, she was my mother's friend, and if I didn't answer, my mom would be on the phone in thirty minutes wondering why.

Pushing the door to Reid Real Estate open, I hit the

green button to answer the call and lifted the phone to my ear, shooting Amanda a smile. "Mrs. Wellington, what can I do for you?"

"Cameron!" Her shrill voice almost made me pull the phone from my ear.

Instead, I gritted my teeth, smiled at my realtors, and took to the stairs. "Yes. Mrs. Wellington? Is there a problem with one of the houses?"

"What's the planning permission on the second house you showed us? Can we put in a pool?"

Oh, fuck me. Like the private stretch of beach wasn't enough for Her Ladyship. "I just this second walked back into the office—why don't you give me an hour to check up on that for you and I'll call you back?"

"An hour? I don't have an hour, Cameron. Do I have to call someone else?"

I knew damn well that she wasn't going to call anyone else, and so did she. But still, I played along. "Of course not." I took the second set of stairs up to my office, keeping my head down. "You know I'd get them right away, but Mayor Green's son and his wife are moving back to town, and I have a meeting with Mrs. Green in ten minutes to get her some information."

There was a pregnant pause, then, "Of course. Mayor Green can't be kept waiting, and neither can his lovely wife. Why don't you send me that information to my email when you've got it today? I do appreciate all your hard work."

Imagine that.

"Not a problem at all," I said, walking into my office and pushing the door shut. "It's my pleasure. I'll talk to you soon."

"Thank you for all your wonderful work today. The houses are simply gorgeous."

Casey came to the door, eyebrows raised.

I frowned. "Of course, Mrs. Wellington. Goodbye."

As soon as she said her goodbye, I hung up.

Casey stormed in and slammed the door behind her. "I thought your viewing was this afternoon?"

"Andrew Lockart canceled, and Antonia was able to come out early. What's the problem?"

"The problem?" she hissed. "You bailed before I could introduce you to Mallory so I had to ask Mom to look after Tilly until three! Poor Mallory had to deal with Jemima Carlton while I was pumping in the kitchen!"

That was almost enough to put the fear of God in me. Jemima Carlton was a lioness on the best of days.

"Did she survive?"

"Oh, she survived," Casey said with a snap. "Apparently, Jemima demanded to be put through to you, but she either has grandparents as eccentric as ours or a closet two-year-old at home because she soothed her enough to get her to call back tomorrow. And. You. Were. Not. Here." She jabbed her finger in my shoulder with every word.

I held up my hands. "All right, all right. Why don't you go calm down, and I'll come to meet her officially in a second?"

"I don't trust you, so no. I'm bringing her in here."

Before I could say a word, Casey stormed out of my office and turned toward the desk.

Shit.

I was in trouble.

I took a chug of water from the bottle on my desk and stood, straightening out my suit. Regardless of anything, I was still the boss here, and I'd get her back at some family function sooner or later.

I followed Casey out into the hall. The woman I assumed was Mallory was sitting behind the desk, looking up at her and nodding.

Dark brown hair fell in curls over her shoulders, and her attractive features gave her the perfect profile—the kind of one a kid in school made silhouette artwork out of. Pouty lips, a button nose with just the right amount of curve on her nose, and a sleek jaw that was currently slightly dropped as she took in whatever Casey was telling her.

She nodded again, her hair bouncing as she did so, then paused. As if she could feel my eyes on her, she turned her head toward me and met my gaze.

She was fucking beautiful.

Her dark-blue eyes widened, recognition and panic flashing in them, and her cheeks flushed pink in a wave that started at her neck and finished at the top of her high cheekbones.

Hell, I think it ended at her hairline—half of which was obscured by bangs that swept over her forehead in a style similar to Casey's.

Speaking of… My cousin's eyes flitted between us for a second before she stepped forward. "Cameron—Mr. Reid—this is your new assistant, Mallory Harper. Mallory, this is Mr. Cameron Reid."

Mallory stood slowly, her cheeks still flushed. It took her a good moment to meet my eyes again and hold my gaze. When she did, though, all hints of recognition and shyness were gone.

In their place was resolute determination.

She put her hand out in an offering. "It's a pleasure to meet you, Mr. Reid."

I couldn't help the slight upturn of my lips as I took her hand in mine. She had a surprisingly firm handshake, but I couldn't tell if that was her actual handshake or her gripping onto me for dear life.

Either way, it was endearing.

"The pleasure is mine, Miss Harper. Or would I prefer

that I call you Mallory?"

"Mallory is fine." Another blush colored her cheeks as she dropped her hand, but it seemed as though it didn't bother her. "Unless you'd prefer Miss Harper?"

I wanted to grin at the glint in her eye. It was almost…challenging. "Well, you're not my insufferable cousin here," I said, eyeing Casey.

She rolled her eyes.

"Oh, you're cousins?"

I raised my eyebrow. "Case, I know you generally try to claim you were adopted, but didn't you think that was important?"

Casey didn't bat an eyelid as she straightened a file on the desk. "Not at all. Like you said—I claim I'm adopted on a regular basis. Especially in the last few months, given your propensity to fire all your assistants, I chose to keep it quiet this time."

Mallory's lips curled to the side, and she dropped her gaze for a heartbeat.

My cousin side-eyed me for a second before turning her attention to my new assistant. "Mallory, I'm terribly sorry I didn't tell you that this hunk of frustration is related to me by more blood than I care to admit. By all means, feel free to throw the sugar in the trash and skimp on the sweetener, too."

It was incredibly hard to be professional around her.

"Casey, you can go now."

"But I was just getting started."

"Weren't you just complaining about the fact Aunt Moira has Tilly until three?"

"Well, yes, but—"

"Mallory and I will be just fine." I gave her a pointed look. "I know you'll be back here tomorrow morning to make sure I haven't fired her, so..." I made a walking motion toward the door, hoping she'd get the hint.

She did.

That was why she was wearing a huge, shit-eating grin. "All right. Let me run things over with Mallory one more time, and then I'll be out of your hair, *cuz*."

"I think she's probably got the hang of it. She looks smarter than the last girl you hired."

"Maybe you should hire your assistants yourself."

The phone rang, cutting through our childish banter. Mallory grabbed for it like it was her lifeline out of here, and with a perfectly friendly tone, said, "Good afternoon, you've reached Cameron Reid's office. Mallory speaking. How can I help you?"

As she slid into the cushy leather chair, I motioned for Casey to follow me toward my office. "Do you have to be such a shithead?" I hissed her.

"Yes. If you'd had an older sister, she'd be doing this."

"You're a month older than me. She's just fine.

Look at her. Now go look after my niece before I invest in ten years' worth of drumsets for her." I gave her a hard look before I slammed my office door and sat down in my chair.

My heart was racing, and it was fucking stupid. Casey had made me look a fool in front of my new assistant, and the longer I sat in silence behind my closed door, the angrier I felt. Most of my staff were used to our tempestuous, sibling-like relationship, but it wasn't the impression I wanted to imprint on my new assistant.

Especially not one as beautiful and familiar as Mallory Harper.

How the fuck did I know there? I couldn't imagine a situation where I couldn't remember meeting her.

Rubbing my hands over my face once again, I pictured hers.

That dark hair that sat in loose curls around her face. Big, dark-blue eyes. Bee-stung, pouty lips slicked in red lipstick. Cheeks pink like my grandmother's roses.

A knock sounded at my door, and I sat up straight, instinctively adjusting my tie. "Come in."

The door creaked open, and Mallory peeked inside, holding a coffee mug in her hand. "Am I interrupting anything?"

Yes. Thinking about you.

"Not at all," was what left my mouth.

She smiled, her entire face brightening with it. "I checked your schedule and saw that you're free. Cynthia Carlton asked that you return her call as soon as you had a moment, if it was sooner than first thing tomorrow morning." She hid a laugh. "I thought I'd bring you a coffee before you tackled that conversation."

"I appreciate it, thank you." I moved the dirty coffee cup from this morning so she could put the new one down. "I'm sorry she was one of your first conversations today."

"Oh, it's fine." Mallory took the dirty mug without batting an eyelid. "If you think she's hard work, you should meet my great aunt." She shot me a smile before pausing at the sound of the phone. "I should get that. Sorry."

She darted off, leaving my door ajar before I could ask her to close it.

Oddly enough, it was only at the sight of her leaving that I froze, my memory flashing with the events of two days prior.

A beautiful brunette woman, on her ass on the curb. Her Starbucks cup flattened on the sidewalk with the hot, fresh coffee splattered over the concrete, and big, dark-blue eyes staring up at me with pure embarrassment.

Holy shit.

The crazy woman who'd run in front of my car was my new assistant.

And, no matter what she'd said, after meeting her, I had no doubt in my mind that those flamingo panties had been hers.

There was only one word for this situation.

And that word was: fuck.

FIVE

MALLORY

I'D BEEN STARING AT THE CLOCK FOR FIFTEEN MINUTES, JUST WAITING
for the big hand to tick up to the twelve. The little hand
had been firmly edging its way toward the five for far
too long.

I needed to get out of here.

This new job was a disaster.

Meeting my new boss—Cameron Reid—had been
nothing short of utterly embarrassing. After Casey had
introduced us, I wanted to run and hide in the bathroom
and attempt an escape out of the window.

I may well have done if I'd had my purse with me.

Thankfully, I'd been saved by the bell. The phone, if
you wanted to be entirely specific. It'd pulled my attention
away from the hottest man I'd ever met—who'd almost run

me over and was now my boss.

Up close, he was even more handsome.

I mean, it wasn't like I was able to share unashamedly at him when I was on my ass on the curb, was it? I'd been so humiliated I'd wanted to run away, and I'd done it. Complete with a portion of my ass on show.

Today, I had no escape route, and I'd had no choice but to make eye contact with him numerous times.

All I had going for me at this point was that he hadn't recognized me. Not yet, anyway, and I hoped like hell it stayed that way.

The last thing I needed my new boss to know was that I was a complete and utter walking disaster. Much like sex, that was something you saved for later on in a relationship. Like when I was six months in, and he liked me to enough to not fire me for being a hot mess.

Granted, I probably couldn't keep my disaster tendencies under control that long, but I only needed this job for three months.

I could do that. I could totally not screw this up for three months so I could move out of my parents' place.

Setting attainable goals and all that.

The big hand ticked onto the twelve, and I grabbed hold of my mouse so hard I almost crushed it. I took a deep breath and made sure I had all the programs and files saved and shut down before I turned off the computer.

It would be just like me to accidentally delete everything.

Then I'd have been screwed. It'd taken me weeks to get this job. I'd need to start praying to get another if I lost this.

With another deep breath, I made sure I had all my things and headed for Mr. Reid's office. I knocked on the door, holding my purse against my body like a shield.

A clunk came from inside, followed by some gentle scraping, and I heard a deep hum of agreement as the door opened.

He stood on the other side, phone to his ear, and waved me in. "I'll call you back," he said into the phone before he tapped the screen and put it down.

"Am I interrupting?"

"Not at all. Just a friend." His blue eyes darted to my purse. "Are you done?"

"It's five," I said, clutching the strap of my purse tighter as butterflies swilled in my stomach. "I was just checking if you needed anything before I left."

"Is it? Crap." He checked his watch. "Well, I'm running late," he said with a chuckle. "I'm all good, Mallory, thanks. See you tomorrow?"

I nodded. "What time will you be here?"

"Around ten-thirty. I have an early viewing." He

paused. "Would it be wrong of me to ask you to get me breakfast and put it in the fridge?"

Uh… "Depends. Do I have to cook it?"

He laughed, his whole face lighting up with amusement. Pressing a hand to his stomach, he said, "No, you don't have to cook it. Just go into Java Hut and pick it up. I'll call ahead of time and pay for it."

"I can do that." I smiled. "Is that everything?"

He nodded once. "Thank you. I appreciate it. I'll see you tomorrow."

I stepped out of his office with another smile. "See you tomorrow."

"And, Mallory? Good job today. It takes a saint to put up with my cousin for that long." He grinned right as his phone rang again.

Dipping my head, I smothered a laugh. "She said the same about you. Goodbye, Mr. Reid."

I dropped my hand from the door and headed for the stairs, feeling his eyes on me long after the phone had stopped ringing.

With any luck, he was looking at my ass and not trying to figure out if he knew me from somewhere.

And there was something I never thought I'd think.

Me: I can't take this house anymore.

I SLUMPED FORWARD ON THE TABLE IN THE KITCHEN. GREAT AUNT Grace and Grandpa had been going at it for two hours, and not even Mom was hiding the Jack Daniels anymore.

Nope. The bottle was open in the center of the table, and she was nursing a glass of the amber liquid like it was a newborn baby. For real—if this carried on any longer, she was going to put the bottle down her shirt or some shit.

"Six hours," Mom said in a tired voice. "They've been fighting for six hours. We went for a late lunch at the garden center because your grandfather slept through lunch and they argued the entire time. First, because he'd slept through lunch and Grace was hungry. Then it ended up with them bickering because Grace said he was an old coot who needed to be put down like a dog, then they fought because apparently, she'd once run over his dog who'd then needed to be put down."

My phone buzzed with a text as she continued to complain about their arguing.

I was starting to wonder what was worse: the arguing or her complaining about the arguing.

Jade: Wanna come over?

Me: Can't. I have to work tomorrow, remember?

Jade: Oh yeah. You're a real grown-up again.

Me: Don't go that far.

Jade: I wanna hear about your day. I'll bring wine.

I eyed Mom's bottle of Jack.

Me: You should probably bring Mom some Jack.

Jade: Is it your relatives or the lack of sex she's struggling with?

Me: I'm not talking about this.

"Mallory, are you listening to me?" Mom snapped her fingers in front of my face.

I looked up from my phone. "No. I tuned out around the dog thing."

She sighed, pouring herself another glass.

"Shouldn't you slow down? Don't you need to cook?"

Mom glared at me. "You can cook."

"That's debatable," I said slowly. "I can cook, but I'm not particularly good at it."

"Even you can make chicken pasta, Mal."

"Again, I can, but that doesn't mean it'll taste good."

"What did I do in a past life to get stuck with this mess of a family?" She got up, sighing, and shoved her chair toward the fridge. Stepping up onto it, she leaned over it and stretched her arm, reaching into the gray box that housed the potatoes.

"Mom," I scolded her, noticing the familiar box in her hand. "You're not smoking again!"

She held one finger to her lips and tapped a cigarette out of the box. I pressed my fingers to the center of my forehead as the strike of a match filled the air.

The acrid scent of cigarette smoke filled the kitchen as my mother moved toward the sink. She leaned forward and pushed the window open, then bent over the sink and blew smoke out of the window.

"Why don't you just open the door and smoke outside? It's bad enough having the choo choo train in the living room without you as well." I waved my hand in front of my face.

She glared at me and opened the back door, stepping out into the yard instead. "I swear this is my house."

"And I'm paying you rent," I reminded her.

"You're giving me a hundred bucks a month, Mallory."

"Do you want me to be able to move back out or not?"

She pursed her lips together before taking a long drag on the cigarette and turning away from me. I'd offered to pay more, even before I'd gotten my new job, but she'd refused.

She couldn't play that card.

At that moment, there were three loud knocks, and the front door swung open. From where I was sitting, I could see the hall, and I grinned at the sight of my best friend.

Jade was tall, loud, and didn't give a damn what anyone thought of her. Right now, her violet hair was pulled into a high ponytail that swung with every step she took, and her bright-pink lips were stretched into a smile as she waved two bottles of wine.

"I brought presents!" she sang, kicking the door shut.

"Is that Jade?" Mom asked, craning her neck to see.

"Who else walks into this house with wine and announces herself with a song?" I asked dryly.

Jade grinned, sashaying her way into the kitchen. She stopped dead when she saw my mom smoking. "Helen! Is that a cigarette?"

"No," Mom said, moving her arm so it was out of sight.

Sure. She had a problem with Jade seeing her smoke, but not me.

I shook my head as Jade put both bottles on the table and grabbed three glasses of wine as if she lived here. Without being asked, she poured three full glasses—not the shit they poured in restaurants—and handed them out to us.

"Now," she said, sitting down. "Tell me about your

new boss."

I groaned, cradling the glass with my hands. "Remember the other day? When I had my interview?"

"Yeah. You were almost run over by a really hot guy because you were in La La Land." She tapped her nails that were as purple as her hair against the table. "What about it?"

I stared at her.

She darted her brown eyes to look at Mom. "What?"

"He's my new boss," I muttered, immediately swigging from my glass.

Silence, and then—

Mom burst into laughter, leaning against the doorframe to steady herself. "The guy who almost ran you over is your new boss? How does that happen?"

"The universe hates me? I don't know. I didn't ask."

"Did you mention it?" Jade asked, grinning. "Because that's funny."

I shook my head so emphatically I swear I heard my brain rattling. "No. I most definitely did not tell him. He didn't mention it either, so I think he doesn't recognize me."

"How can he not recognize you? He could have killed you."

"I don't know. I don't have bright purple hair?" I shrugged. "Trust me—when you're as hot as he is, a regular-looking brunette like me is nothing special."

Jade rolled her eyes as Mom shut the back door. "Regular looking? What are you, Susie from the Walmart counter?"

"She may as well be if she's got a crush on her boss," Mom mused. "Nothing good ever comes from fantasizing about your boss."

I balked. "Who said I was fantasizing about my boss?" My voice was squeaky. "I've only spoken to him twice. Three times max. I'm not fantasizing about him!"

Not yet. I mean, the job was still new and the night was still young. Who knew what stupid thing I'd do next?

Mom sighed and shook her head, picking up the glass of wine Jade had poured. "Not yet. That doesn't mean you won't. Working with someone you want to sleep with isn't a good idea."

"Speak for yourself," Aunt Grace said in a husky voice, shuffling into the kitchen. "I once worked with a hot as hell contortionist, and let me tell you, that was a damn good idea. The positions that man could get his body into would have made the person behind the Kama Sutra blush."

Jade hid a smile behind her glass.

"I don't think there was a single person behind the Karma Sutra," Mom said.

"You'd know, hussy," Aunt Grace shot back. "Have you been smoking again?"

"So, tell me about the job." Jade quickly steered the conversation back to me. "The job, not the boss you'd like to climb like a tree."

I glared at her. "It's good. He was out for most of the day today so it was quiet. He seems to deal with the richer clients, judging by the properties I was pulling today."

Sensing that their argument was no longer of interest to us, both Mom and Aunt Grace disappeared into the living room.

"What kind of rich are we talking?" Jade leaned forward when they'd gone. "Pretty rich, or richy rich rich?"

"Bit of everything," I said slowly. "Why? Are you looking for your third boyfriend of the year?"

She stuck her middle finger up at me. "Mark was never my boyfriend, and Adrian was a jerk. I just didn't know it until he told me it was time to dye my hair."

Yep. That was how my best friend rolled. The only person who was allowed to tell her to do something was, well, me. Even then, it was debatable if she'd listen.

"But, seriously. Does he need another assistant? I'm a little worn out at my job," she said, referring to her job as a hair stylist at the only salon in town. Well, the only one I could afford, anyway. "People are tiring."

"You'd be worn out at the grocery store," I pointed out. She was a lot like me in the idea that she was still figuring out what to do with her life.

We were twenty-five. We probably should have figured it out by now, but nobody was perfect.

"Yeah, whatever." She waved her hand. "So, what are you going to do now that Mr. Dreamboat is your boss?"

"Uh, work?" I raised an eyebrow. "That weird thing I'm paid to do? I know that's a hard concept for you to grasp every time Mrs. Tolstoy comes into the salon with the latest gossip she overheard at the bar, but some of us do still do it."

"Oh, pish." She snorted and tilted her glass in my direction, eyebrows raised. "I work. One day you've got Mrs. Tolstoy coming in for her new color with who said what at the latest coffee morning at the church, and the next you've got old Alberta Hennington for a perm and all she wants to talk about is her newest bunion. I take my kicks where I can get them."

"Like imagining me fantasizing about my hot new boss?" My eyebrow stayed in its raised position.

"Exactly like that."

"Well, let me tell you," I said slowly, looking her dead in the eye. "That isn't going to happen."

Jade leaned back, smiling behind her glass. "Famous last words, Mallory. Famous. Last. Words."

SIX

MALLORY

JADE AND HER 'FAMOUS LAST WORDS' COULD BITE ME. AND WHEN SHE was done biting me, she could kiss my ass.

Twice.

My morning had started precisely how I'd thought it would. Apparently, when I'd set my new alarm, I'd forgotten to set it for every day.

That was right. I was so bad at adulting I couldn't even set the alarm correctly.

Anyway. I'd woken up forty minutes late, meaning my hair that needed a wash was now pulled back into a sleek ponytail, and I'd dry shampooed the shit out of the pony in the hopes nobody would notice it was just this side of leaving a grease stain on my shirt.

All right, so it wasn't that dirty, but it probably wasn't

that far off, either.

If it couldn't get any worse, there was no coffee thanks to my mom's horrific hangover, and on the way to work, I'd stopped off at my usual coffee shop.

Completely forgetting that Cameron Reid had asked me to grab his breakfast on my way in. Of course, that was something I'd forgotten until I was already in the office and behind my desk, so I'd had to run back out.

He was, just now, walking in the door, and I'd been back all of five minutes.

At least I'd been able to grab another coffee when I'd picked up his food.

Silver linings and all that.

"Morning."

I smiled up at my new boss. He was wearing the same, hot as hell light-gray suit he'd worn each time I'd seen him. "Good morning, Mr. Reid."

He quirked a brow, his lips tugging to one side. "You can call me Cameron, Mallory. I'm not my father."

I blushed. "Okay."

"I have to make a quick phone call. Would you mind making me a coffee and bringing it in with my breakfast, please?"

"Not a problem." I got up, almost knocking the keyboard off the desk. I slid it back, not willing to make eye contact with him.

It was too soon for him to know he'd hired a total klutz.

"Thank you," he said, amusement tingeing his tone. "I'll leave the door open for you."

I nodded, not looking up until I knew he'd disappeared. My cheeks were burning—over a goddamn keyboard.

This wasn't going to end well, was it?

Making sure not to touch anything else, I edged my way into the kitchen and shut the door behind me. As the coffee machine whirred to life, I removed his bagel from the fridge and stared at me.

He'd need a plate, but was I supposed to take it out of the paper bag?

Oh, crap. This was a nightmare.

I stared at it. Surely he didn't want me touching his food. I didn't want to touch his food.

Wait—why was this an issue? It was a bagel, not his damn penis.

I put the bag on a plate, shaking my head, and fixed his coffee. Why the hell was I so nervous? It was coffee and a bagel. Was it because of the whole almost running me over thing?

He was kind enough, from the few words we'd exchanged. With any luck, there would only be a few words right now, and those would be, "Hi, thank you."

I was never that lucky. My name literally meant 'unfortunate.'

I stirred the sweetener into his coffee and grabbed both the mug and the plate. Somehow, I managed to make it through the door and across the office hall to his open door without tripping over my own feet. God only knew my stomach was flipping uncomfortably with nerves, so that made it an even greater feat.

At my high school graduation, I'd been so nervous I'd tripped over nothing. Literally nothing.

Peeking around the door, I saw that Cameron was no longer on the phone. "Knock knock."

He looked up, eyes brightening when he saw me. "Come in. Thank you. I'm starving." He moved a folder on his desk for me to put his things down. "Oh, good. You left the bagel in the bag. One girl kept taking it out, and I had to fire her when I saw her use her nail to scrape earwax out of her ear."

I shuddered, taking a step back. "Don't worry—I promise to always bring it in a bag and never pick my ears."

He laughed, sipping his coffee. "How's the morning been?"

"Quiet," I replied, clasping my hands in front of me. "Two phone calls. One from a Mrs. Townsend whose husband is looking for a house with an outdoor workshop and some land. She didn't have a budget as she was just looking for a ballpark."

"Did you send her any?"

I nodded. "I sent her every property for sale with at least an acre of land and either the outdoor workshop already in place or with a structure that could be easily converted."

"Great." He pulled out the bagel. "Who was the second call?"

"Oh, uh, my mom."

"Is everything okay?"

"Not if you live in my house right now," I muttered.

He raised his eyebrows in question.

"Um." I laughed nervously. "My grandfather and great-aunt are here for his eightieth birthday. They're…temperamental."

Cameron laughed quietly, wiping the corner of his mouth. "That explains so much."

"I'm sorry?"

"Yesterday." He paused. "Casey said you'd had a call from Jemima Carlton and had managed to convince her to call today. She said you either had a toddler or demanding relatives. Something like that."

"Oh." Now, it was my turn to pause. "Jemima Carlton. Shouts a lot, right? Lost the ability to use the word please after the first sentence?"

He winked at me. "That's the one."

"Well, I can't wait for her to call back." I tried my best to keep the sarcasm out of my tone, but I didn't do a very good job if Cameron's low chuckle was anything to go by.

As if on cue, the phone rang, and his chuckle became an all-out belly laugh. "Looks like you've tempted fate."

I pursed my lips, giving his handsome face my best unimpressed look, and went back to my desk to answer the phone. "Good morning, you've reached Cameron's Reid's office at Reid Real Estate. Mallory speaking, how can I help you?"

"Good morning, darling! This is Jemima Carlton. We spoke yesterday." Her nasally tone was utterly grating, and I had the urge to offer her a tissue to blow her damn nose.

"Oh, good morning, Mrs. Carlton!" Despite the fact I hadn't wanted to speak to her, Cameron had forgotten one small point when he'd laughed when the phone had rung: she wasn't calling to speak to me. "What can I do for you today?"

"I've taken a look on that website you've got thanks to my grandson, and I'm extremely interested in that lodge in the mountains. Is it still available?"

"Great," I replied. "Can you give me the name and I'll bring up the information?"

"Barfield Lodge."

"Two seconds, please." I brought the information up on the computer and looked. I found it quickly, thanks to it being the only lodge available. It was beautiful, set in its own pocket of snowy wonderland. "Yes, it's available."

"Wonderful!"

I swear, she clapped.

"Is darling Cameron available? I'd love to discuss a viewing."

I bit my lip. "I can arrange that for you, Mrs. Carlton."

"Oh no, darling. He handles me personally."

Thank Heavens for small mercies.

"Let me put you on hold for a moment, and I'll see if he's free." I pressed the button and put down the phone before she could say anything else.

Getting up, I made my way to Cameron's office just in time to see him pick up his cell and put it to his ear.

I folded my arms over my chest, smirking. "I just saw you pick that up. I know you're not talking to anyone."

He groaned, putting it down. "It's her, isn't it?"

I nodded. "She wants to look at the Barfield Lodge. I offered to arrange the viewing, but apparently, you deal with her 'personally.'"

Sighing, Cameron met my eyes. "Patch her through."

I grinned, turning around with a bounce in my step as I went back to my desk and picked up the phone, hitting the hold button again. "Mrs. Carlton? Mr. Reid is available. I'm putting you through now."

I tapped the button to redirect her call to his line before I had to listen to her nasal tone again. There was only so many times you could hear a sound that felt like nails down a chalkboard before you wanted to rip out your own eyes, no?

Day two, and I was already starting to wonder if I was cut out for this job.

I wasn't exactly a people person. Especially not at the grocery store, because the doors are *not where you have a fucking conversation.* Neither is the middle of the aisle.

I digress.

I put the phone down and sat back at my desk. My bottle of water was still ice-cold, and I sipped as I checked the email account. There were a few unread ones, so I worked my way through those, then moved to familiarize myself further with the properties on the books.

I worked quietly for an hour, answering the phone whenever it rang. It wasn't until the sensation of being watched crawled over my skin that I finally stopped and looked up.

Into the perfect blue eyes of my boss. And he was grinning. A big, bright grin that made him ten times more handsome.

That sigh? It was my ovaries.

"Sorry. I didn't want to interrupt you," he said in a low voice.

"Oh, um. It's okay." My traitorous cheeks flushed lightly. "I was just—" I paused to wave the information on an eye-wateringly expensive house I was reading. "Catching up on some information."

Cameron walked over and took the paper from me, leaning on my desk. "Starting at the most expensive end, I see."

"Yeah," I replied slowly. "I'm a little torn between imagining myself winning the lottery and buying this house or hating the people who can." I tilted my head to the side. "I'm in a relatively good mood right now, so I think I'm on the lottery side right now."

He laughed.

"Do you need anything?"

He smiled at me. "Yes—I have a phone call in around ten minutes. Could you order lunch from this deli?" He handed me a flyer I hadn't realized he was holding. "They do the best sandwiches, and they'll deliver them."

"Sure." I looked down at the flyer. "How do I pay them?"

"Tell them you're calling from my office and they'll add it to the tab. Ask them for my usual, and they'll sort it out and deliver it." Cameron stood, then stopped, looking back over his shoulder. "Hey, Mallory?"

I held the phone in front of me. "Yes?"

"Do you have plans for lunch?"

"Avoiding my mother who I know is downtown with my aunt," I replied. "Why?"

"Why don't you order yourself something and we'll eat

lunch together?"

"You want to eat lunch with me?" I blinked at him.

"You seem to have the hang of this job," he said with a shrug. "And, hell—you've already lasted longer than the last girl."

"It's my second day."

"Exactly." His lips twitched to one side. "Order yourself something, and when I'm done with my call, we'll take lunch."

He disappeared into his office and shut the door before I could argue with him.

Great.

Lunch with my boss.

My boss who was hotter than hell and had almost run me over less than a week ago.

I glanced at the listing for the multi-million-dollar house and snorted as I pushed it away.

I was definitely broaching on hating the people who lived there now.

SEVEN

MALLORY

IF YOU'VE EVER THOUGHT THAT HAVING LUNCH WITH YOUR BOSS AFTER two days would be weird, you would be correct.

Especially a boss who was as hot as Cameron Reid was.

Now, look. Don't judge me. I knew that eyeing up my boss was, quite frankly, an absolutely fucking stupid idea. The problem was, I was a woman, and I had a little thing called hormones going on.

Do you know what the problem with hormones is?

They have a mind of their own.

So today, my hormones didn't care that the walking hunk of hotness opposite me was my boss. Nope. They just wanted to crawl across the table and climb him like a koala.

Nom nom nom. Right up the abs that I imagined were behind that starchily-pressed white shirt and perfectly-tailored gray jacket.

Like a ladder. Ab by ab by ab.

Jesus, I needed a life. And some help. Professional help.

And a blindfold so I stopped staring at my boss like he was a pepperoni pizza and I was on a low-carb diet.

Not that I'd ever do that, you know. I liked carbs too much. My ass could tell you that much. I was *this-close* to busting a seam on my jeans.

Maybe. I mean, I couldn't really see my ass in jeans, but the possibility was always there.

"So, what happened with your last job?" Cameron asked, wiping the corner of his mouth with a napkin. Those bright blue eyes focused wholly on me. "Casey called for a reference, and your boss was more than willing to give you one."

I sighed and sipped my water. "He retired. He's pretty old. To be honest, he gave us a lot of time to get new jobs, but I just wasn't lucky."

"How about your colleagues?"

"You mean my tall, thin, blonde-haired, blue-eyed colleague who could charm a condom onto a monk?"

"That's an interesting way to describe someone."

I snorted into my hand. "Sorry. My brain can't always define between boss and friend."

"Carry on. By all means, you're a breath of fresh air." He laughed, folding the napkin and sitting back. His lips were curled into an unfairly delicious smile.

Shit. I needed to eat this sandwich before my hormones took control of my brain. It was bad enough that my brain was in control of my brain.

I smiled behind my hand. "Well, not everyone likes my brand of fresh air."

"Fresh air is overrated." He smirked. "Tell me about your family. I think you mentioned a crazy aunt and grandpa?"

"That's a rabbit hole you do not want to go down," I warned him. "Do you always talk this personally with your assistants?"

"No. But considering that I grew up with my only long-term assistant, I'm more than familiar with her weird family." He grinned.

"You make it sound like you're horribly picky with your assistants."

"Worse than Mariah Carey needing tea."

I raised an eyebrow.

"The women in my family outnumber the men. I'm subjected to far too much celebrity gossip when I'm forced to my mother's house."

I wished celebrity gossip was all I was subjected to at my mother's. It was far preferable to knowing—and witnessing—the fact your parents had a more active sex life than you'd ever have.

Not to mention adventurous.

I still wasn't over seeing them doggy-style it on the staircase.

"I admit," Cameron said, picking up his mug of coffee. "I am picky, but I have to be. I like my assistants to be... just so. And, honestly, Casey is a hard person to follow. She's worked here since she graduated high school, for my father before me. She knows the business inside and out."

"What happened to the person who covered her maternity leave?"

"She was from an agency. She was only ever temporary, and I know Casey hoped that I'd hire her, but she just didn't have that...something." He tapped his finger against his chin. "She couldn't handle the clients. This might sound strange, but I'm sure you've already figured out there's a divide in the company."

"You mean you deal with the rich people?"

He barked out a laugh. "Basically. This was my grandfather's business, and all his contacts have filtered down through the generations. Word of mouth is a great thing—if someone is happy with how I broker a deal, they'll pass on my information to someone else. But the clients can be...difficult."

"Like Cynthia Carlton?"

"She's something." He paused, visibly fighting a laugh

if the light in his eyes was anything to go by. "She's hard work, but she means well. She's a good friend of my mother's, and yes, she's challenging. Like my mother," he finished on a mutter.

"You should meet mine," I muttered right back.

"She calls me every morning to see if I ironed my shirts correctly and makes me send her pictures," he drawled. "Being an only child isn't that fun."

"I wish I only had to send my mother pictures of my shirts," I shot back. "I have to set an alarm so they know to stop having sex before I get home."

He froze. "Are you serious?"

"I have endless therapy sessions with a bottle of wine that says I am, sadly, deadly serious." I sighed and cradled my water, having pushed the leftovers of my delicious sandwich out of the way. "It's their... thing."

"I am far more thankful for my parents now," he said, lips twitching. "Is it better now that you're working?"

"It's better because my kooky relatives are in town," I replied. "My great-aunt is a walking, chain-smoking, whiskey-drinking menace, and she loves nothing more than to argue with my cigar-loving, scotch-downing grandfather."

"Are they related? Blood, I mean? Or marriage?"

"Blood. Brother and sister." I wrinkled up my face and checked the time. "I should clean this up and get back to my desk."

"I got it." Cameron stood with a half-smile, gathering up the wrapping from his sandwich. "Get yourself a coffee and go back."

"Oh, it's fine. I can—"

"Mallory, despite what my cousin may have told you, I'm not a dictator. I can clear up sandwich wrappers, especially when having lunch together was my idea. My mother raised a gentleman."

My cheeks flushed. "I didn't mean—um, I wasn't trying to say that…"

He laughed, tossing the ball of the wrapper into the trashcan. "I'm teasing you. I'll clean up. You get back to work." He threw me a wide grin that held more than a hint of charm in it.

Still, I balled my wrapper up and threw it in the trash. "There. Now I don't feel so bad."

Another laugh escaped him, and he pushed my bottle of water across the table to me right as my phone rang.

He raised one eyebrow. "Looks like your lunch hour's up."

Ugh. Amanda didn't miss a trick.

I wanted to sigh, but I had no time. Instead, I had to rush over to my desk in my heels, almost tripping on the way there. If it weren't for the desk being within reaching distance, I'd have fallen flat on my face.

Thank Heavens for small mercies. Like desks. And closed doors, so Cameron had never seen me trip.

"Good afternoon, you've reached Cameron Reid's office. Mallory speaking. How can I help you?" I breathed, trying to steady myself.

"Mallory?" Great Aunt Grace's voice harped at me down the line. "Is that you?"

I slumped again the desk. "Aunt Grace. You know I'm at work?"

"Did I call your work phone?"

"Yes."

"Then I know you're at work, child."

I gritted my teeth. "What do you need?"

"We're out of strawberries."

I froze. Was she for real? She called to tell me we were out of strawberries? "Seriously?"

"Yes. There are none, and I made pancakes for lunch. I wanted chocolate sauce and strawberries with them."

"We...don't have chocolate sauce either, Aunt Grace."

"Oh." There was a brief pause. "Then I guess I need chocolate sauce and strawberries."

"I'm at work." I rounded my desk and sat down. "I can't run to the store for you right now. You'll have to make more tomorrow."

There was a crash from the other end of the line.

"Aunt Grace, what was that?"

"Nothing!" she shouted. "I found the sauce. We're good! You work hard, babykin!"

Babykin? What the fuck was babykin? And why was she calling me it?

"Aunt Gra—" I was cut off by the line going dead. A deafening beep sounded in my ear, and I groaned.

Goddamn it, Aunt Grace.

I put the phone back into the cradle and tapped the keyboard to wake up my computer. Strawberries and fucking chocolate sauce. How did she even get my work number? How did she even know where I worked? I was pretty sure I'd never given that information up.

Not to her, at least. There was no way I wanted her showing up here with a random idea. She might have only been here two weeks, but people could lose a job in two minutes.

I didn't want her to be the reason I lost mine.

"All right?" Cameron asked, adjusting his black tie against his white shirt as he walked toward my desk. "Anything important?"

"Is my aunt asking me to get her strawberries and chocolate sauce counted as important?" I asked honestly, meeting his eyes.

His lips twitched. "Is she buying a house to eat those in?"

"I'd prefer she didn't buy one in the area."

Cameron turned toward his office, laughing. "Nope, not important."

As he shut his door behind him, I couldn't help but laugh myself.

He wasn't wrong.

Me: I need a new job.

Jade: Why? What's wrong with urs?

Me: My boss is too hot. I keep thinking about him with his shirt off.

Jade: Do I need to hire u a stripper?

Me: For what?

Jade: U need to get laid.

Me: Strippers don't sleep with you, idiot. Hookers do that.

Jade: K. Do u need a hooker then?

Me: No. I need some self-control. And Aunt Grace to not email me @ work to buy her strawberries.

Jade: Oh God. Did she get a hooker?

Me: You're impossible. Why do I put up with you?

Jade: I bring u the good wine when ur sad. Do u need the good wine?

Me: I always need the good wine. Srsly, my boss is too good to be true. He bought me lunch today.

Jade: Maybe he's just being nice. U should try it.

Me: Being nice is overrated. And he probably is, but he's too perfect.

Jade: ?????

Me: He's hot as fuck and buys me lunch and wants to get to know me and doesn't want to get in my pants. What's wrong with him?

Jade: Is he gay?

Me: I doubt it. But if he is, men have a gift I don't

think they deserve.

Jade: K. Maybe he fancies u.

Me: I don't think so. Maybe he just bites his toenails?

Jade: Only u could go from something hot to something so gross.

Me: It's totally probable. He has a tab at a deli on the fancy side of town. The only tab I have is my credit card.

Jade: U have one at HLS.

I groaned. Hook, Line, and Sinker was our local dive bar, and we loved it for the cheap drinks and the world's best wings. We frequented it far more than I cared to admit, and because the owner, Hank, was a softie, he let us open tabs.

Mine was definitely due.

I made a mental note to pay him the next time I walked through the door.

Me: So do you. Hank knows I'm good for it. But that doesn't solve my super-hot-boss problem.

Jade: Uve worked there for two days. Settle ur tea kettle, Mal.

Me: Fine. You come meet me for lunch tmrw. See how you feel about him.

Jade: It's a date. I bet he's not that hot.

Me: Twenty bucks says you're wrong.

Jade: I've seen ur exes. Done.

EIGHT

CAMERON

I PUSHED OPEN ONE OF THE HEAVY DOORS THAT MADE UP THE ENTRANCE to my parent's house. As always, I cringed at the ostentatious show of wealth on display, from the perfectly polished marble floors to the oversized diamond chandelier that hung in the center of the hallway.

If you asked my mother, she wasn't showing off.

She merely liked shiny things.

I'd told her before that only worked with magpies and toddlers, but she'd stuck to her guns thus far.

For what it was worth, I really did think she just liked shiny things. She also had the bank account to have lots of shiny things.

"Mom?" I called into the silent house. "Where are you?"

"Mrs. Reid said to tell you she's in the study." Isabelle, the full-time housekeeper, appeared from the living room to my right with a duster in her hand. "And you're late."

I chuckled at her stern look. "I know I'm late. She's lucky I'm here at all if she keeps sending her friends to buy houses from me."

Isabelle rolled her eyes and smiled. "And what would you do if she didn't, huh?"

I reached and took her hand. "I'd be able to have time to romance you, Isabelle."

She barked a laugh and snatched back her hand. "I'm sure you would, Cameron. There's nothing like a woman in her forties with a teenage son to get a young man's motor running."

"Aw, come on. You could get anyone you wanted."

"Yeah? Do you have Chris Pratt's phone number?"

"If I did, I'd set you up myself." I grinned. "How is Oscar?"

Her face lit up as it always did when she spoke about her son. "He's doing well! I was wondering… when you're settled with your new assistant…"

I smiled, knowing what she was going to ask me.

"Oscar needs work experience for extra credit, and he's interested in what you do. Would you—uh…" She stumbled over her words.

Saving her, I touched her shoulder and smiled.

"Isabelle, of course. I'd love to have him with me. How long is his experience?"

"One week. Five days, technically."

I nodded my head once. "You have my number. We'll figure it out." I squeezed her arm.

"You're a good boy, Cameron. Now scoot before your momma catches you messing around out here."

I laughed, letting her go back to work, and headed down the hallway to my mom's study. My shoes squeaked against the impossibly clean floor, and if I looked down, I could see my reflection on the tiles.

My mother was a slave driver.

She'd have a fit if she saw the spaghetti stain on my living room floor that was currently being masked by my coffee table and a well-placed ottoman.

It was also why she wasn't allowed to my house.

"You have a crease in your shirt," she said, her shrewd blue eyes raking over me the second I stepped through the door. "It's unbecoming of a young man."

"It's good to see you, too, Mother," I said dryly. My hand smoothed over the spot on my shirt she was staring at. "How are you?"

"As bored and as intolerant of fools as ever."

"That explains why Dad isn't here." I bent and kissed her cheek.

Her lips curved to one side. "Don't let him hear you say

that. He's at the cabin for a few days to make sure he's got everything ready for hunting season."

"Hunting season doesn't start for another month."

"So I keep telling him, and so he keeps ignoring." She rolled her eyes and slipped her glasses on top of her head. "How is work?"

"Work is fine," I said slowly. "Keeping busy, thanks to your long stream of clients you keep sending my way."

She waved a hand, her perfect manicure flashing through the air. "People always need houses, darling. You just happen to be very good at making people buy the ones they don't think they need, but actually do."

"I don't know. I'm not entirely sure Cynthia Carlton needs another house in the mountains."

"Robert's company had a breakthrough, and the value soared practically overnight. Doubled his wealth," she mused. "And I'm sure they'll sell the old one when she's found a new one she likes."

"Just like a pair of shoes."

"Exactly. She's frivolous. Goodness knows what she'd ever do if they lost all their money." She shook her head. "Anyway, how is your new assistant? I had coffee with Anna yesterday, and she said Casey liked her a lot. And do sit down, Cameron—you're making the place look untidy."

I swallowed back a sigh and took a seat in one of the cream leather chairs. "She's doing really well, actually. I was shocked at how competent she was given that I almost ran her over a few days ago."

Mom choked on her coffee, almost spilling the hot liquid over her white pants. "You did what?"

"Well, it wasn't me. Harold Bridgerton wanted to view a house and insisted on driving, and from what I understand, she stepped out into the road, and his driver slammed on the breaks." I shrugged a shoulder and leaned back. "Total accident."

"I don't think having someone you almost ran over working for you is a good idea."

"It's fine, Mom. She doesn't recognize me, and if she does, she hasn't said anything. Besides, she's good at what she does. She even handles Cynthia with ease." I rested my foot on my knee. "It's magical."

Mom sniffed. "She hasn't met her in person yet. You'll see if she's cut out for the job then."

Dear God, the woman was hard to please.

I shook my head. "Was there a reason you called me today?"

"There's always a reason, Cameron. Why else would anyone pick up the phone?"

"To talk?"

"And that is the reason," she replied wryly. "But yes, there is a reason behind my call. Your grandfather wants to downsize, and he wants you to find him a new house."

"Why can't he call me himself?"

"You know what he's like. Ever since he discovered that Chess website, that's all he does."

Ah. The Magnus Carlsen site where he can play people online. Yup. It was somewhat of an addiction.

"Anyway," Mom said. "He's getting a little old now, so he can only really have one floor. No stairs, a low-maintenance yard, and I'd like him to be a little closer to us so I can check on him more often."

"Not a lot, then."

"Don't sass me, Cameron."

I sighed. "Mom, why don't you find him a place, and I'll sort it out from there?"

"Because you're the realtor, and I'm retired." She sniffed, eyeing me. "Do you not want to help your grandfather?"

Dear God, the woman could get a murder confession out of the weapon if she really wanted to. "I didn't say that. I just thought that since you knew better than I did what he should have…"

She raised one plucked eyebrow, the same shade of dark brown as her hair.

I knew that look.

That was the 'Shut the Fuck Up, Cameron,' look.

"Never mind," I said, gripping the arms of the chair. "I'll have Mallory search our listings tomorrow. I'm pretty sure one of the girls downstairs has a few properties in her books that will fit what Grandad needs."

Mom nodded. "Stay for dinner."

"I…"

She raised her eyebrow again.

I sighed inside. Yep. I should have known better than to try to leave. "Sure," I said. "What's for dinner?"

MALLORY CLICKED HER TONGUE AS SHE LOOKED AT THE COMPUTER screen. "Stupid thing. Stupid piece of—"

"Everything okay?" I asked, eying her from the door to my office.

She turned to me, her dark-blue eyes wide. "Oh, um, yeah." Her cheeks flushed the way they did whenever I caught her unawares.

It was weirdly adorable.

"Computer giving you trouble?" I sipped my coffee, keeping my eyes trained on her.

She tucked a wisp of hair behind her ear, ducking her head and glancing at the screen. "A little. It keeps freezing, and I have a client asking about properties that I need to respond to."

I strolled over to her and set my coffee on the empty

coaster. "Let me take a look." Leaning over her, I grasped the back of her chair and took the mouse from her. My fingers brushed hers, and she drew in a short, sharp breath at the touch.

I resisted the urge to look at her and focused on the computer.

There was no denying that Mallory Harper was beautiful. It'd been my first thought when I'd seen her lying on the sidewalk with her coffee cup flattened behind her.

Her brown hair was curly but pulled up into a bun on top of her head. Random strands fell out and curled around her neck and ears, and it was one of those that curled around her ear that bugged her.

She pushed it back again, her knuckles brushing against my chest as she did so. Visibly leaning away from me, she focused intently on the screen.

Her eyelashes were stupidly long. They curled right back so they almost brushed the skin beneath her eyebrows with each blink, and she puckered her full, red lips more than once.

God only knew red lips were my weakness.

They couldn't be on my assistant. Could I enforce a dress code of no red lipstick? Fuck knows she was hot enough to be a weakness.

Instead of focusing on the way she looked anymore, I swallowed hard and scanned my gaze over the computer. It was frozen, so I did a hard reset.

"Did Casey say the last time she'd done any checks on it?" I asked, shaking the mouse as it loaded up to make sure it was working.

"Checks?" Mallory asked, her voice fading. "What checks?"

"Virus scanning, defragmenting, things like that."

"What's defragmenting?"

Dropping my chin, I let out a small laugh. "It's a process on the computer that scans it and pulls back together fragmented parts of files."

"That...helps."

Another laugh escaped me as I tapped the keyboard for her to log in. "Files break up, and defragmenting is basically the process of the computer finding those pieces and putting them back together again."

"Ohhh. Okay. That makes sense."

I smirked as the home screen came on and I took back control. "I assume Casey told you absolutely nothing, then."

"Nope. Not a damn thing."

"All right. Let's fix this thing." I brought up the virus scanning software, trying my best to ignore the way she shivered when my arm brushed hers.

Click. Click. Click.

I set the software doing its own thing and stood back a little. Mallory blew out a long breath and settled back into her chair. The phone rang, the high-pitched sound exploding through the silence of the room.

She scrambled to grab it and held it to her ear, giving her now-familiar greeting. She even said it all with a smile on her face, a fact that made her words sound all the brighter.

"Absolutely, Mrs. Cavendish," she said, grabbing a notepad and scribbling on it. "My system is currently down for some routine maintenance, but as soon as it's back up and running, I'll make sure to send the information for the property to your email... No, it shouldn't be long. It'll be by the end of the day, absolutely... Wonderful. Thank you so much for understanding."

I waited until she finished the call and said, "You know, you can use my computer while I'm doing this."

"Oh—it's okay. I mean, I've told them, so..."

I stood back as the bar ticked closer to being done on the virus software. "Mallory, it's fine. You can log in to your profile on the system on it." I rested against the desk and shrugged. "I'm not using it if I'm fixing your computer. Honestly, go. This could take a while. I don't need it right now."

She bit the corner of her lip, and I almost expected her lipstick to scrape off, but it didn't. "Are you sure?"

"Absolutely sure. Go use it." I waved my hand in the direction of my office. "Go get your emails sent out. I can handle this."

"Don't you have an I.T. guy for this?"

"Yes, but he's my cousin, and he smokes a little too much weed to be employable," I mused, taking her seat as she stood. "If it weren't legal, we'd all be in trouble."

She covered her mouth with her hand, and I was pretty sure she was hiding a laugh. "Thank you," she said, casting a glance over her shoulder as she made her way to my office.

"You're welcome." I watched her as she went, appreciating the way her skirt hugged her ass.

Look. I was a human. My assistant was hot—I'd already established that, and it wasn't a crime to eye up someone who worked for you.

Morally wrong, perhaps, but not illegal-wrong, so whatever.

I rubbed my hand down my face and shook my head. Jesus. I needed more coffee if I was justifying staring at my assistant's ass.

Turning my attention to the computer, I watched as the virus software did its thing and checked the files for anything. When it was done, it'd found a few questionable things, so I set it to clean up and moved to the defragmentation software.

That would take all damn day.

The only thing Casey knew how to clean was a tiny human's butt.

An excellent skill in itself, but that didn't help run my business.

I sighed and watched as the computer began the process of cleaning itself up. There was nothing more to do here, so I got up, tucked the chair in, and made my way into the kitchen.

Shit. I had no idea how she took her coffee.

And why the fuck was I making coffee? That wasn't my job. That was why I had an assistant. With a great ass.

Double shit.

I shook those thoughts out of my head and walked to my office. She was sitting in my tall leather chair, typing diligently without looking at the keyboard. It was an impressive skill, especially with how quickly her fingers moved across the keys.

I waited until she stopped and clicked, then said, "Hey—I'm making coffee. Do you want one?"

Mallory looked at me with wide eyes. "You're making me coffee?"

"Well, I did take over your computer. I figure that caffeinating you is the least I can do."

"I'd be more annoyed if this chair wasn't so damn comfortable." She wriggled in it just to make her point. "Also, your computer is ten times faster than the dinosaur out there."

I leaned back. Maybe it was a bit of a dinosaur as far as

technology went. "I'll see what I can do about that. It's probably time for a tech update. My dad bought the last computers, and he knows as much about them as my mom does physics."

"Does she know anything about physics?"

"Not a damn thing," I replied. "Your computer is doing its thing, but it's gonna take a while. Feel free to work in here for now. The only problem might be your phone."

Not that I'd have a problem with watching her run over to her desk every time it rang...

"Oh." She sat up a little straighter at that. "I can reroute the calls to yours and answer here."

"What if it's a personal call?"

"Is there anyone calling you I shouldn't be talking to? Wife? Girlfriend?" She raised one eyebrow.

I coughed. "No. Nobody like that. Just my mom."

She grinned, her eyes lighting up with the movement. "So someone I shouldn't be talking to?"

"On the contrary, please do. I'd rather you talk to her than me." I paused. "Speaking of, she wants me to find a new place for my grandfather to live. Could you search our listings through the entire company and see if there's anything that fits her particular demands?"

"Sure. What are they?"

"One floor, no stairs, low-maintenance yard, and relatively close to her house so she can visit."

"Where does she live?"

I gave her the address.

She whistled. "Does she have a budget? Buy or rent?"

"Buy," I replied. "And you heard that address. Do you think she has a budget?"

"No." She fought a laugh as she met my eyes. "Never mind. I got it. I'll ask Amanda and take a look. Anything else?"

"Yes. How do you take your coffee?"

"How I take my men. Tall, dark, and not nearly as sweet as I should." Mallory paused. "In fact, my track record dictates a change. Toss in some cream and two sugars."

"My mother cleared out the sugar."

She turned her attention to the screen and said, "Casey told me where you hide the sugar. I take sugar, not that sweetener crap. There's enough sourness from my great aunt."

I laughed as I stood up. Damn. I liked her more and more every single time she opened her damn mouth.

She was a keeper, that was for sure.

NINE

MALLORY

I BLEW OUT A LONG BREATH AS CAMERON LEFT TO MAKE COFFEE.

My mother had been right. Working with a guy you were attracted to was a terrible idea. I'd never tell her that, of course, but she was right.

It was only—what? Day three? And it was already becoming a problem.

The worst part was that I was sure he knew I was attracted to him thanks to my shiver earlier when he'd touched me.

My body had given me away more than once in that conversation, and now I was sitting here, on his very comfortable chair, and I was totally sure that I could feel the imprint of his ass on the seat.

I wriggled.

Yup.

There it was.

It was a nice imprint.

I sighed and focused back on my work. I didn't have to wait long for my coffee because Cameron brought it back a few minutes later. I smiled at him as he set it down on a coaster.

"Thanks," I said, reaching for it. "Are you sure me using your computer isn't a problem? Don't you have work to do?"

He waved one large hand and sat in the chair on the opposite side of the desk. "Nothing I can't do later or at home. Besides, I have a viewing this afternoon, so I won't be here later."

"Oh. Are you—"

"Mallory. I'm sure." His lips quirked to the side. "Honestly."

"Okay." I blushed and set the mug down.

Except I didn't.

I missed the edge of the coaster.

Cameron jumped back before I even knew what happened.

The mug tipped right as I let go of the handle, and scalding hot coffee burst all over his desk. It coated sheets of paper and a red, cardboard folder and everything inside it. Dark spots splattered over the edge of the desk to the floor, and a leather-bound diary was swimming in what was once my coffee.

I clapped my hands to my mouth and froze. My eyes darted back and forth over the mess I'd accidentally created.

This was it.

This was the moment he realized he'd hired a total klutz.

"Oh my God," I whispered, slowly dragging my hands away from my face. "I'm so sorry." I couldn't even look at him. "I'll get a towel—or three. Maybe a wet cloth. And a trash bag. I—"

"Mallory." Cameron caught my wrist before I could rush out of the office.

A tingle ran up my arm from where he was touching me, and I swallowed hard before I met his eyes.

A hint of amusement gazed back at me. "It's fine. It was an accident. Stop panicking."

"I know, but all your work, and—"

"There's nothing there that can't be printed out again. It just means you have extra work this afternoon." He gave me a lopsided grin. "Honestly, it's fine."

Groaning, I dropped my head. "I'm such a klutz."

"Yeah, but I knew that when I saw you on the side of the road on your ass."

I groaned again. "I was hoping you didn't recognize me."

He laughed, letting go of my wrist. "Not a chance in that. Come on. We can get this cleaned up in no time if we work together."

I followed him out of the office. "You don't have to help me."

"No, I do. There's still a cup of coffee in that office. I don't want you turning mine into a casualty too."

Ugh. This was terrible. "I wouldn't blame you if you fired me. I'm a bit of a liability."

Cameron laughed and tossed me a towel from the bathroom. "Mallory, I'm not going to fire you for spilling coffee. It missed the computer, didn't it? It didn't go on me. Nobody got hurt, and nothing blew up. Don't be so dramatic."

"I can't help it," I muttered, following him back to the office. "It goes hand in hand with being a walking disaster. Eventually, you do something worth being dramatic about."

"Have you done that?"

"Done what?"

"Done something worth being dramatic about."

Yeah. I was inadvertently responsible for an apartment fire.

Instead of saying that out loud, I swept my arm out in front of me, indicating the coffee. "Is this not worth being dramatic about?"

"Not at all." He picked the leather diary up. "I liked

this, but I can buy a new one." He put it in a trash bag I didn't know he'd grabbed. "The paper? It can all be printed out again. You just need to write down what it is so you know what to print."

"Right. Um." I looked around and saw a notebook—under the coffee. "There's a problem."

"There's a pad in the drawer. It's college-ruled. Are you likely to make a disaster of staying between the lines?"

I jerked my head up, ready to be offended, but a smile was tugging at his lips and his eyes were bright with laughter.

He was teasing me.

"Ugh." I opened the drawer and found the notebook he was referring to on the top. I pulled it out and paused because the movement had revealed another notebook beneath it.

It was bound with gold rings and covered in high heel shoes.

"Um," I said, fighting laughter as I removed that one, too. "Is this yours?"

Cameron paused his cleaning and eyed it. "Uh, no. That's my ex-girlfriend's."

"How much of an ex is she?"

"Enough of one that it shouldn't be there. You can throw it in the trash."

I looked at the drawer. "Did you also know there's a

half-empty packet of gum in there? Plus, a pink highlighter, a sock, and a razor."

"What sock?"

"I don't know. I'm not touching your sock." I handed him the girly notebook, and he tossed it into the trash bag. "What do I need to print?"

Together, methodically, we worked to clean the desk. Well, mostly Cameron worked. I wrote down everything he told me I needed to print out again while he cleaned everything up and threw out the stuff I'd ruined.

I had a list as long as my arm to print back out, and I was pretty sure I'd need to go and get some more ink when I grabbed lunch with Jade, but after almost an hour of organizing and wiping everything down, we were done.

"Hey. Are you ready for lunch?"

I jolted at the sound of Jade's voice. She was hovering at the top of the stairs and could see me since I was level with the doorway of Cameron's office.

"Hey," I said, smiling. "Give me a minute. I need to finish up here then get my phone sorted."

"You're good," Cameron said, tossing the towel into the trash bag. "We're done. It's all cleaned up, and I can always answer the phone."

"Are you sure?"

"Clean up? What did you do?" Jade was already hiding a laugh, and she tucked a wisp of her violet hair behind her ear as she walked toward me.

"I...spilled some coffee," I said slowly.

"Some?" Cameron chuckled, shaking his head. "Try a whole mug."

"A whole mug? Holy shit, Mal—what did you do? Miss the coaster?" Jade asked, coming to the doorway.

"I—yeah." I sighed.

Cameron laughed again and held a hand out toward Jade. "You must be the best friend. Are you as much of a klutz as she is?"

My cheeks flooded with embarrassment as Jade all but froze on the spot. She looked Cameron up and down, very obviously, and grinned.

"Nobody is as much of a klutz as Mallory, and I've seen her great-aunt drunk. Jade." She smiled as she shook his hand.

"Cameron." He took his hand from hers and turned back to me. "Go take your lunch. It's all good."

I hesitated.

He gently pushed me in the shoulder. "Go. Oh, can you get some printer ink when you're out? I don't know what it is, but..."

I half-smiled. "I'll call Casey and find out what it is. She gave me her number for this reason."

"Yeah, and so she can gloat at me for weeks." He sighed. "Go on, go, before I change my mind about you calling her."

"Are you sure? I can do the phone, or help you finish up here, or—"

"What's that?" He pointed to the glass of water on the desk.

"It's a glass of water."

He stared at me.

"Right. Got it." I grimaced and waved the notebook. "I'll just put this on my desk. Don't touch it."

"You'll probably lose it on the way."

I gasped. "I'm a klutz, not a forgetful toddler."

Jade grinned. "Well…"

"You shut up." I pointed at her and stalked toward my desk. I set the notebook down next to the keyboard and checked the screen. There was some weird program full of colors and graphs and stuff that I didn't understand. After a brief frown, I grabbed my phone and my purse and turned to Jade. "Let's go."

"All right." She tugged her purse strap onto her shoulder and bounced toward the door. "Let's go!"

I pulled my purse straps up to my elbow and poked my head in the door to Cameron's office. "Do you want me to get you anything when I'm gone?"

"Nope, I'm good." He smiled, his bright eyes shining. "Have fun."

I smiled back and turned, walking to Jade and urging

her down the stairs. We'd barely taken a step when she leaned into me, grabbing my shirt, and said in a low voice, "Damn girl, he is fine with a capital 'F.'"

A huge laugh came from inside Cameron's office, and my jaw dropped at the knowledge he'd heard what she'd said.

Even Jade's eyes went wide. "Let's get lunch."

"Mhmm."

"HOLY SHIT, HE'S HOT."

I rolled my eyes. It was the third time she'd said that since we'd sat down in the diner and ordered.

She'd said it twice before we'd ordered, and three more times on the way.

"I know," I said simply, reaching for my milkshake. "I have to look at him on a regular basis."

She slumped forward and rested her chin in her hands. "He's so beautiful. Like a sculpture in an art museum. Totally beautiful. Like someone picked all the best parts of a man and put them all together."

She finished it off with a sigh.

A long, dreamy sigh that wouldn't be out of place in a Disney princess movie.

"He's also my boss," I said slowly. "Doesn't matter how hot he is. You can't drool over him like he's a pizza on cheat day."

"Can I use him for masturbation material?"

"No!" I pinched the bridge of my nose. "Jade…"

She pursed her lips. "All right, all right. But I do not promise anything."

I rolled my eyes and sipped my milkshake. "I told you he was hot. But he's still my boss, so that's the end of that."

"Not for me."

"Yes, for you. No great love stories start with screwing your best friend's boss."

Jade paused. "There are plenty that start with screwing your boss, though."

"I am not going to sleep with my boss. Cut that out. And I wouldn't say there are any great love stories that begin with anyone having sex with their boss."

"That's how my mom met my dad."

"All right, so your parents are an exception to the rule." I sighed as our food was brought over and deposited in front of us, the waitress pausing to see if we needed anything else. When we said we didn't, she left us with a smile.

"My parents have been happily married for years. It's totally possible to have a happy ending with your boss."

"Are you trying to marry me off to Cameron?"

"There's nobody else knocking at your door."

I dipped a fry in ketchup and pointed it at her. "You don't exactly have a long list of gentlemen knocking at yours, do you?"

"No, but this is why I keep Logan around. I'm not ready to commit." She shrugged a shoulder and picked up her burger. "I don't need a long list. Plus, I'm not a romantic pansy like you."

I laughed. "What, because I like romance movies and books, I'm a romantic pansy?"

"No, the endless doodles over your notebooks in school proclaiming you Mrs. Nick Jonas are."

"Hey." I pointed another fry her way. "I would husband him so hard if I could. Some things don't change, and my love for Nick Jonas is one of them."

"Well, I admit, I didn't see it then, but I do now." She shrugged. "Puberty did that man good."

I slowly nodded after biting into my burger. It most certainly had. Then again, it'd done me more than a few favors, too. Puberty and braces, that was.

We finished our lunch in relative silence after that, only casually throwing out little bits of conversation until we were done, and we'd paid.

I held the door open for her to walk through. "Are you going back to the salon?"

Jade nodded. "Need an appointment?"

"Yeah. Can you text me? I have to get some printer ink so I can print out all the stuff I ruined."

She smirked. "At least now, he really knows you're a catastrophe."

I shot her a dark look as we parted. "Not funny!"

TEN

MALLORY

Cameron: Sorry I missed you this afternoon. Did you get all the stuff printed out?

I STABBED SOME PASTA WITH MY FORK AND HIT 'REPLY' ON THE SCREEN.

Me: Most of it, but I think a couple of the properties have sold since they were printed.

"Are you texting at the dinner table?" Grandpa peered over the table at me as he picked up his whiskey. "You kids these days. You have no respect."

Mom side-eyed me, begging me not to say anything.

"It's my boss. Would you prefer if I left the table to have my conversation?" I asked in the sweetest voice I could muster.

Grandpa frowned at me. "Are you sassin' me, girl?"

"No, she's not sassing you, you old coot," Aunt Grace snapped. "She can't ignore her boss, and it's rude to leave the table before you've finished eating."

"It's rude to text at the table," Grandpa shot back at her. "Especially with your elders."

Mom grabbed her glass and downed it.

My phone beeped, and my fingers twitched with the urge to pick it up and read the message. I resisted it, instead turning it down so the screen was flat against the table and I wasn't being tempted by it.

Instead, I tapped my fingers against the table and turned my attention to eating.

"The phone shouldn't even be there," Grandpa continued. "I told you that kids have no respect. In my day we sat and ate and talked about our day."

Oh, Jesus. This was going south fast.

"Well," Dad said, politely wiping his mouth, "It's a little different now, Eddie. Phones at the dinner table are normal."

"It's rude."

"So are you," Aunt Grace griped. "You're not letting anyone eat. You're not talking about your day. You're just bitchin'."

"Enough." Mom held up her hands and stopped the

conversation before it got any worse. "Yes, texting at the table is bad manners, and Mallory has now stopped. If anyone would like to begin a civil conversation about their day, do it now."

Nobody said a word.

"That's what I thought." She double-checked her glass to make sure it was definitely empty then sighed. "Everyone just eat."

We did as we were told. There was silence for the rest of the meal—if you ignored Grandpa's quiet muttering under his breath to himself, that was.

It was awkward and uncomfortable, but so were all family gatherings. I much preferred the ones where I could simply show up for a couple hours and then disappear.

The ones where the family stayed here? Not my favorite.

Dad finished first and got up, taking his plate with him. It was the cue we all needed to move, and although Mom and I moved to clean up, Grandpa and Aunt Grace didn't.

Grandpa disappeared into the living room, and Aunt Grace took to the hallway where her purse was.

There was the sound of a door closing and shutting, and Mom looked toward the front door with a glare. She wouldn't go far—she was too old for that—but there was no doubt she was going for a little walk to cool off.

Dad wrapped his arm around Mom and whispered

something in her ear. She deflated but gave him a weak smile and nodded. He squeezed her lightly before letting her go, and Mom crossed the kitchen, pausing to kiss the side of my head.

I waited until she went, then said, "Is she okay?"

Dad shook his head as he opened the dishwasher. "She's stressed. Having your aunt and grandpa in the house twenty-four-seven is getting to her. They're picking at just about everything. Your grandpa complained there was one half-dead leaf on the plant earlier."

I picked up a plate to scrape the leftovers in the trash. "She knows what they're like. She didn't have to have them stay for a week if she didn't want them to."

"I know that, but you know how she can't say no to them."

"I'll arrange it next time. Everyone will be on vacation." I scraped the last plate off and carried them over to Dad.

His lips twitched and took the plates from me. "Good thinking, sweetie. Until then, can you leave your phone in your room at mealtimes?"

"I have a better idea," I said brightly. "How about I just don't eat here until they've gone? Everyone wins."

"Can I join you for that dinner?"

"How about me, you, and Mom go out, and we leave the skeletons to fend for themselves?"

He choked back a laugh and almost dropped a glass.

"Okay, I don't need to tell you that you shouldn't call your relatives skeletons."

"But I'm going to anyway."

"And after the past few days, I'm not going to confront you about it." Dad chuckled, putting the last of the dishes in the dishwasher. "We can't leave them alone. They'll burn down the kitchen, and we've had enough fires in this family for a while, thank you."

I rolled my eyes and grabbed a wet cloth to wipe the table. "That was a total accident, and you know it."

"I do." He grabbed me and kissed my hair. "I can take care of this. Go get your phone and talk to your boss. You've kept him waiting long enough."

"It's nothing important. I just had a little accident at work, and he was gone when I got back from lunch. He's just checking in."

"Oh no. What did you do?"

"Spilled coffee. Hot coffee." I paused. "Thankfully, on the desk, not him, and a miracle made me miss the electronics."

He chuckled quietly, pushing the dishwasher closed. "Now there is a miracle if I've ever seen one. I can finish the kitchen. I get a break from the skeletons—your mom doesn't. Go do your thing."

"Hey. Why can you call them skeletons but I can't?"

He shrugged. "I pay the bills. Now, before you go—I

told your mom to take a hot bath. Take her this." He grabbed the bottle of Jack and filled a glass almost to the brim. "Tell her to not put a ton of water in."

I laughed and picked it up, then grabbed my phone. "Gotcha. Thanks, Dad." I darted away before I was caught up in anything else.

It took me only a few seconds to get up the stairs and knock on the bathroom where Mom was running a bath. "Mom? Are you good?"

The lock clicked, and she opened it to reveal her wrapped in her fleece robe. "What's up, honey?"

"Dad sent this." I handed her the full glass of Jack.

She smiled, taking it from me. "Thanks, Mal. Sorry I haven't been nice."

I waved a hand. "Nah, it's okay. I mean, Grandpa's here with his ornery self, and Aunt Grace is a pain in the ass, and if you discount those entirely, I totally disrupted your sex life, so…"

"That's enough!" She laughed, moving to shut the door.

I stepped back, laughing, and let her do just that. She clearly needed her own time, so I crossed the hall and went into my room with my phone. I was finally able to bring up my last message from Cameron, and I unlocked my phone as I jumped onto my bed.

Cameron: They probably were. It's been a while since I organized that desk.

Cameron: Hello?

I snorted.

Me: Sorry. Grandpa took offense at 'kids these days' using their phones at the dinner table. And by a while, do you mean a year?

His response came a lot faster than I thought I would.

Cameron: Sounds like my family dinners. And yeah, a year is about right...

Me: Do you need me to sort your desk out?

Cameron: Is that an offer to remove all my ex's shit from my office?

Me: When did you break up?

Cameron: 18 months.

Me: It's not an offer. I'm going to sort your desk out so hard tomorrow. That is ridiculous.

Cameron: All right, all right. I officially put you in charge of sorting out my office. Bring your rubber gloves.

Me: Is it that bad? Should I stop by the store for cleaning supplies?

Cameron: No, but we might be out of milk…

Me: Milk and rubber gloves, then.

Cameron: Now that's work talk.

Me: I'll even answer the phones in between.

Cameron: Carry on.

Me: I'll pour you coffee and call you Mr. Reid.

Cameron: Is it too early in this working relationship to say that was kind of professionally hot?

I laughed, dropping back onto my bed so my head bounced off my pillow.

Me: Maybe. Maybe not. Who has to get breakfast from the deli tomorrow?

Cameron: …I want to say me.

Me: No. Totally not too early. What time can I expect you?

Cameron: Oy.

Me: Oy?

Cameron: One half of 'oy vey.' It's when you're too professionally hot for me to finish a sentence.

Me: It might be too early for a line like that.

Cameron: Alrighty then. I'll be in just after you at nine.

Me: I like cream cheese bagels with ham and coffee and cinnamon rolls.

Cameron: It's too early in this professional relationship for you to demand things.

Me: Next time you're in and Cynthia Carlton calls, I'm patching her right through.

Cameron: Cream cheese bagels with ham and coffee and cinnamon rolls it is.

Me: Hahahaha.

Cameron: I'll make sure there's a lid firmly on your coffee so it doesn't explode everywhere this time.

I stared at my phone screen. He was my boss, but what a smartass fuck he was.

Me: Next time I'll spill it on you. And it won't be an accident.

Cameron: I don't keep spare pants at the office.

Me: Why do I need to know that?

Cameron: Casey once brought Tilly to the office and there was a vomiting incident. She needed to know.

Me: I'm not a newborn likely to vomit on you.

Cameron: You just threatened to toss coffee on my pants. I thought you should know so we don't find ourselves in a position where I'm wandering around in my underpants.

Me: …Bring extra pants.

Cameron: I'm not three. I don't need extra pants.

Me: Ok. So I need to buy extra pants. What size are you?

Cameron: This is entirely too personal.

Me: Does Casey know?

Cameron: 34 waist and as long as possible in the leg.

Me: I'll bring the pants and you bring the breakfast, and I'll sort out your entire desk.

Cameron: Can you leave your best friend at home this time? I'm not a steak, and she looked at me like a T-Rex eyeing up a triceratops.

Me: Science says a T-Rex wouldn't attack a lone triceratops. Horns and all that.

Cameron: How do you know that?

Me: Netflix.

Cameron: I don't know how to respond that.

Me: Cream cheese bagel with ham and coffee and a cinnamon roll.

Cameron: If you don't show up tomorrow wearing rubber gloves, I'm not handing over your breakfast.

Me: If we weren't mere days into this I'd threaten to show up in a lot less than rubber gloves.

Cameron: ...I don't think it's safe for you to wander around in your underwear.

Me: Me either. So I'll see you in rubber gloves with milk in my hand.

Cameron: And I'll bring you breakfast and coffee... with a lid.

Me: Ha. Ha. Ha.

Cameron: See you tomorrow, Mallory.

Me: See you tomorrow, Cameron.

ELEVEN

MALLORY

I PULLED THE OFFENSIVELY YELLOW RUBBER GLOVES FROM MY PURSE AS
I headed up the stairs. They were seriously uncomfortable to wear, but a deal was a deal, and I was really in the mood for a cinnamon roll.

The tension had still been rife at home this morning before I'd left, and I'd taken an extra long shower this morning to avoid having to spend time with my family, save for the kiss I'd dropped on my mom's cheek before I'd left.

I couldn't believe they were barely talking to each other because of one text message.

I snapped the second glove on and scanned the office. I'd waited until now because I hadn't wanted anyone to see me wearing them—I was pretty sure my colleagues downstairs already thought I was a little weird. There was no need for them to have that idea totally confirmed.

Cameron wasn't here yet, so I set my purse behind my desk and shrugged off my blazer. It was warm as hell in here, and it only took me ten seconds to decide to lean over and let some cooler outside air in.

The window swung open far faster than I thought it would, sending a gust of air hurtling in and knocking a stack of papers off my desk. I stopped, legs as far apart as I could get them thanks to my dress, with my arms out, one toward the fallen papers and the other toward the window.

The phone made my decision for me.

I snatched it up. "Good morning, you've reached Cameron's Reid's office at Reid Real Estate. Mallory speaking, how can I help you?"

"Good morning. I'm interested in the property you have on Canyon Close. Would I be able to arrange a viewing for this week?"

"Absolutely," I said, dropping to the chair and grinding my teeth as another gust came in the window and scattered the papers across the office even further. "Let me open the diary and see what Mr. Reid has available. Do you have a particular day you'd prefer? Times?"

I rested the phone between my ear and shoulder and simultaneously reached for the window and the diary.

"Wednesday, during school hours."

"Right, okay. Two seconds please."

The damn window wouldn't shut. Stupid old fixtures.

I yanked on it as hard as I could while also flipping the diary pages and trying desperately not to drop the phone. I finally got to Wednesday on the calendar, quietly thanking the powers that be that I knew this property because I was the one who'd put it on the website two days ago.

The powers that be obviously thought I was a fucking smug idiot because right then, the phone slipped.

Reflexively, I caught it, trying not to exhale with relief.

Unfortunately, I was no longer alone.

Cameron was here, complete with coffee and a white paper bag that smelled like heaven, and he was silently laughing his ass off at me.

I gritted my teeth and motioned to the window. "Mr. Reid has an opening at eleven o'clock. Does that work for you?"

"Absolutely," said the voice on the end of the phone.

"I'll just need your name and details, and your email address if you'd like me to send you directions to the property."

Cameron set down the bag and coffees and slipped behind my desk. His fingers brushed my upper back as he scooted past me to handle the stupid window.

I busied myself by gathering their details and read their email address back to them before hanging up and dropping my head to the desk.

"What's this? Hurricane Mallory blowing through the office?"

"Ha ha ha," I muttered, sitting back up and spinning to look at the closed window. "How did you—what?"

"Shut the window? Yeah, that one's awkward. I'm shocked Casey didn't tell you. Open the one on the left instead. The hinges on the other one get stuck all the time, and I've just never gotten around to getting someone in to fix it." He dropped his eyes to my hands. "Nice gloves."

"I told you I'd wear them." I got up and knelt to the floor to gather up the papers the wind had thrown everywhere.

Cameron stepped over me to get the ones out of my reach and put them on top of the pile. "And I got breakfast." He pointed to the bag. "Here's your coffee."

"Thank you." I took it from him and sipped as he emptied out the food.

"How did you get those gloves in here? Did you wear them all the way here?"

"Yes. I decided that was the final nail in the coffin of my sanity, and if I was lucky enough, I might just get picked up," I said in a dry tone. "No. I put them in my purse and put them on when I got up here."

"Damn. You strolling through Main Street wearing heels and rubber gloves was a sight I was hoping to see."

My stomach fluttered at that even though I knew he

was teasing me. "Yeah, well keep dreaming."

He handed me a bagel and winked. "I will. Any messages?"

"Nope, but there was already a bite on the house on Canyon Close. They're looking at it on Wednesday."

"That's the new one right?"

"Yeah. We listed it two days ago." I turned on my computer as he set down a cinnamon roll. "It's the one with the old brick façade and the double garage—"

"But only one drive." He snorted. "I remember now. Can you check if there are any permissions needed to extend the driveway? I know everyone is going to ask."

I nodded. "Where do I check that? The Mayor's office?"

"I have the number somewhere. I'll dig it out for you." He pulled one of the waiting chairs over to my desk and sat down.

I couldn't help but raise an eyebrow as he pulled out a smoked salmon bagel and bit into it. "So now we share breakfast?"

He laughed, almost choking on his food. He banged his fist against his chest a couple of times, and a couple of crumbs spilled from his lower lip and over the dark stubble of his jaw to his lap.

He washed a cough away with a mouthful of coffee. "Yes. But, if you notice, I'm far enough away from the coffee in case Hurricane Mallory picks up again."

I pursed my lips and shot him my best glare. "Hurricane Mallory? Really? Is that what we're going with?"

"Do you have a preferred way to describe your…quirky…nature?"

"I don't like it described any way, but if you ask Jade, I'm either a hot mess, a walking disaster, or a catastrophe queen."

"Catastrophe queen." His lips twitched. "Now there's a way to describe you. Do you have a crown?"

"I think I need to look for a new job."

Cameron laughed, dropping his head back.

Damn. His neck was sexy. Just enough muscle and there was a vein that went up the side that looked really kiss—

Wait. No.

Bad Mallory.

"I'm just teasing you. I think I'll stick to Hurricane Mallory. It's accurate enough."

Sadly, it was. Where I went, disaster tended to follow.

"Yeah, well, that's what happens when your parents literally give you a name that means 'unfortunate.'" I pulled my bagel from the bag and tore it in two. "I was never going to be a ballerina, was I?"

His eyebrows shot up. "Really? That's what your name means?"

"Yeah. I've spent a long time wondering if that was how they felt about me, but apparently, my dad has a mild obsession with Mount Everest. He was fascinated by some English guy who climbed it and disappeared until his body was found years later. Mallory was his surname." I shrugged. "If I were a boy, I'd have been George, after his first name."

"Interesting namesake. Usually, it's a book character or movie star."

"Oh, yeah. It gets the conversation going at parties." I laughed. "Bit strange, but whatever. It was a weird coincidence that Mallory means 'unfortunate' and that's pretty much what I am."

He chewed thoughtfully. "I still prefer Hurricane Mallory. That explains the mess of papers on the floor when I walked in. I don't know what describes why you're still wearing those gloves." He grinned, his eyes dancing with amusement.

"Shit." I tugged them off. "Thank God they were new."

His laughter bounced off the walls.

I tossed the gloves in the trashcan behind me and sighed. "See? That's about right for my life."

"All right. Maybe there is a slight unfortunateness to you, but it's weirdly endearing. I'm almost looking forward to what mess you're going to cause next."

"That's the weirdest compliment I've ever been given."

He mock bowed from his seated position and picked up his coffee. "You're welcome. What's on my schedule today?"

We broke from the friendly banter to run through his schedule which included one phone call with the accountant, another with his lawyer about an upcoming buy, two viewings, and not a lot else. After finishing our breakfast and him telling me about two new rental properties that were being photographed over the weekend to go up on Monday, Cameron gathered all the trash from our breakfast and stood up.

And knocked his half-full coffee off the edge of my desk.

I didn't even try to hide my grin as he jumped back to avoid being splashed. He did, but only just, and I laughed as he looked at me and sighed.

"That's karma, isn't it?"

I nodded my head, turned around, and grabbed the rubber gloves from the trash. "You might need these."

"GOOD AFTERNOON, YOU'VE REACHED CAMERON'S REID'S OFFICE AT REID Real Estate. Mallory speaking, how can I help you?" I flicked hair from my eyes and held the phone between my ear and my shoulder as I finished typing an email to the attorney's office.

"Mallory! Is Cameron available?" asked an extremely unfamiliar voice.

I felt like I should know who this was.

"I'm afraid he's out of the office right now. Can I take a message?"

The sigh was massive and should have given away the identity of the caller before she said it. "Yes. Can you tell him his mother called? Again?"

Oh, shitballs.

"Oh, Mrs. Reid, hi. Absolutely. Should I ask him to call you back?"

"Darling, you can ask him to, but that doesn't mean he will." She tutted, and I bit my lip to stop myself from laughing. "Can you pass along a reminder about the mixer tomorrow night at the house? It's imperative that he attends because of his father's future partnership. It should allow us to open an office in Denver."

"Absolutely. Let me write that down for you."

"Seven p.m., but he should arrive at six. His timekeeping skills outside of work are so terrible that he'll likely show up a day late to his own funeral."

This time, I smiled, writing down the times. "I assume he should wear a suit?"

"Darling, have you seen him wear anything else?"

"No, ma'am, but I've only seen him at work." I laughed slightly. "I've written that down, and I'll be sure to pass the message on when he gets back to the office."

"Thank you, Mallory." She paused slightly. "Would you like to come? I haven't been able to get into town and I hear such good things about you. I'd love to meet you."

"Oh, well—"

"I understand it's incredibly short notice, and I apologize, but I know Cameron thinks highly of you and it would be great to have you there."

Whoa. Back up. Back up. Back up.

I was not a person to have at a formal mixer.

I was barely a person to have at a slumber party.

Me. In heels. A fancy dress. Around rich people. Business people. Formally.

Hell. To. The. No.

That was the quickest way to get me fired, let me tell you. I wasn't even allowed to use a straightening iron in my bedroom anymore. I had to use my mom's because that was how much I was trusted, and I was a grown-ass woman… who had every reason not to be trusted with a flat iron, but I digress.

"…Again, it's short notice, and if you have other plans, that's fine," Mrs. Reid continued on. "But it would be wonderful to see you. You should come with Cameron at six so we can get to know each other before the guests arrive at seven."

"I—" Apparently had no words. "Thank you so much, Mrs. Reid. It's a lovely offer—"

"Great!" she said brightly, and I swear I heard her clap. "We'll see you tomorrow night!"

"I—"

The line went dead.

Slowly, I pulled the phone from its cradled position on my shoulder and stared at it.

What the hell had just happened? Cameron might call me Hurricane Mallory, but his mom was a freakin' tornado. I hadn't agreed to go to this fancy mixer tomorrow, but apparently, I was, and I was to go there early to meet his parents and family and act like I knew what the hell to do around people who had more cash in their wallet than I did in my bank account.

In somewhat of a daze, I grabbed my phone and pulled up Cameron's last message to me.

Me: Sir, we have a problem.

Then, I fired one off to Jade.

Me: I just spoke to Cameron's mom on the phone and now I have to go to a fancy mixer tomorrow night.

Unlike Cameron who was at a house, Jade's response vis phone call was swift, telling me she was between clients.

"Are you gonna bone him after?" Was her opening line.

"No!" I said, a little too loudly. "Jade, these people are rich. It's not a casual mixer where you can wear jeans and heels—it's a fucking formal one," I lowered my tone considerably. "It's business. She steamrolled right over me. She may as well have held a chloroform rag over my face and kidnapped me."

"Okay, okay, calm your tits." The line cracked with her heavy exhale. "How fancy are we talking?"

"At least a cocktail dress."

"Okay. You have one of those. You have that red one that makes your boobs look really good."

I frowned. "The one with the flirty skirt?"

"Yep. That counts. It has just enough of a scooped neckline to be like, "Hi, boys," but not so, "I'm charging fifty bucks an hour for this.""

"You have such a special way with words."

"I know. Wear that one with a nice necklace and your favorite black heels. They're broken in, and you know you can walk in them."

"What about a jacket?"

"Wear a blazer. You have, like, fifty. If it's business, you need to be sexy but smart."

"Jesus, I may as well just get some glasses and study up

on physics."

I could almost hear her rolling her eyes.

"Listen to me, Mallory. If you ever bang this guy and you make a good impression now, you're in with his mom. Big win. Moms are hard to impress."

"You have got to give it up with the banging my boss thing. It isn't going to happen. But I'll wear the red dress," I said begrudgingly. "Thanks. I have to go. I don't know when Cameron's getting back and I'm not supposed to be on the phone with you."

"You got it. Go to work, and don't panic. I'll come to do your hair and make-up for you. Let's have lunch tomorrow and figure it out."

I blew out a long breath. "Thanks. Okay, see you tomorrow." I hung up and put my cell down.

With Jade's help, I had half a chance at looking good. Between her and my mom, the possibility was slightly better than half. Before my dad had retired and sold off the majority of their construction business, she'd been used to going to things like this and wandering around, simpering up to people with money who could invest.

My phone buzzed, and I picked it up, seeing that the message was from Cameron.

Cameron: I just got back to the car. What's wrong? Is there a problem at the office?

At the office, on your phone line, inside my head—take your pick, boss.

Me: Your mom called.

Cameron: Nothing good ever comes of that.

Me: I see that. She wanted me to remind you about the mixer at her house tomorrow night.

Cameron: Shit. Is that the problem?

Me: No.

Cameron: Then what's wrong?

Me: She invited me. And I'm not sure how it happened because I don't remember agreeing, but now I'm coming, too.

Cameron: Shit.

Me: Exactly.

TWELVE

CAMERON

"MOTHER!" I PINCHED THE BRIDGE OF MY NOSE AS I PACED MY KITCHEN.
"Why did you invite Mallory to the mixer tomorrow?"

She calmly stirred her tea, not bothering to look up from the cup. It was a teacup and saucer I kept exclusively for her, and she tapped her spoon on the edge of the cup, sending an ear-wrenching clink through the entire room.

"I was being polite, sweetie," she said without batting an eyelid. Her hair was as perfect as ever, without a strand out of place, but that didn't stop her swiping a hand up the back of her bun to push imaginary hairs back into place. "She wasn't invited, and if we open another office, she'll be involved as your assistant."

"How? We work here, not in Denver, and I'm not moving to Denver."

"I didn't say you had to, Cameron. But if we open another office—and it's high time we did—you'll be in control of it and managing. She'll be integral in helping you manage two offices."

I ground my teeth. "You weren't sold on her the other day."

"Well, I spoke her to her, and she called me 'ma'am.'"

"You hate being called ma'am."

"I know, but I like that she was polite enough to do so." She shrugged one shoulder and sipped her tea before delicately setting it back down onto the saucer. "I know that you're trying to put me off inviting her, but I think it's the right thing to do. I'd like to meet her and see if she's up to the job."

Jesus. After the last two days, I wasn't sure Hurricane Mallory was cut out for my mom's kind of mixers. She was exactly how she'd said Jade had described her—a catastrophe queen.

She didn't find disaster. Disaster found her.

"You're not her boss," I reminded her. "I'm her boss. It matters if I think she's up to the job, not you."

Mom waved her hand. "Of course, but we still own the company, darling."

I tried not to grind my teeth so hard that I literally wore them down, but it was damn right. "Yes, but you signed over control of the office to me when Dad stepped down.

My office. My assistant. My choice."

Mom sighed. "I'm not trying to change your choices—"

"You just said you want to see if she's up to the job. You can't decide that in a business mixer where she's not actually doing her damn job. If you want to see that, stop by for a day and see how damn good she is at it."

When she's not spilling coffee or getting the window stuck and wearing bright yellow rubber gloves.

Mom sipped her tea again, not bothered for a second by my words. "Look, I felt rude asking her to pass on the message to you without inviting her. I'd like to meet her, so it kills two birds with one stone."

"She's been there less than a week. You can't expect her to go to the mixer and act like she's been with me for a year."

"I'm not at all. She'll be introduced as your new assistant, but Casey did things like this all the time."

"Casey was born into this job. She was handed the Saturday job as soon as she turned sixteen." I leaned against the island. "She's been in the job for four days. Have you lost your damn mind?"

Mom wasn't bothered at all by my words. "No. I'm quite in control of my faculties, thank you, Cameron."

She could have fooled me.

"Mother. You invited my assistant of less than a week

to a fancy, formal, business mixer. I'd like to argue about the control of your faculties."

"Do you not trust her?"

About as much as I'd trust a landslide in a town center.

"Of course I do," I replied without blinking. "But she's just getting settled. Have you considered that it might be too much for her? She's not as used to this as we are. You have to understand that you can be quiet overbearing sometimes."

Mom paused, turning her eagle eyes on me with disapproval glaring in them. "Does she not want to come?"

"I didn't say that." My words were quick. I didn't want to get Mallory in any trouble, but she also needed to know that she'd overstepped a little. "She's happy to come, but I don't want you putting any pressure on her. She's the best assistant I've had since Casey left, and I don't want to lose her because of this."

Silence reigned for the longest time until she finally sighed. She dropped her shoulders the tiniest moment. "Fine. I understand what you're saying. I advise that you keep her by your side the entire night and lead her in what to do."

"Are you suggesting we throwback to when women were to be seen and not heard?"

"Do you know me at all?"

I quit.

"Support her, Cameron. Professionally, she is your employee, but personally, you are equals." Mom daintily took a drink from her teacup, using both hands to steady the cup. "Show her the ropes. Give her respect. Allow her to speak without overshadowing her."

"Be her boyfriend," I said dryly.

"If that's what it takes to help her through the night, yes. But with less touching."

"Emotion wouldn't kill you," I noted, grabbing my coffee mug to keep me grounded. The woman was a nightmare. "Understanding that she doesn't come from money and isn't used to your soirees would do you well, Mother."

"I know she isn't from money. I did a thorough background check of her when Casey approved her application." Again, another sip from that damn teacup. "She's more than qualified for her position, but is she qualified for this business?"

I slammed my mug down, letting the hot liquid inside splash out onto the island counter, and steeled my gaze against her. "You put me in charge. I say if she's qualified, not you. Even if you say she isn't, it doesn't matter. She's my fucking assistant, and that's all there is to it."

Mom's lips curled up. "I know, I just like hearing you say it."

I'd kill her one day. I could swear it. "Mallory is my

assistant. She'll be there, and she'll do good, even if she has to attach herself to my side."

"I don't want her to attach herself to your side, Cam. I want her to prove she can work for you."

I hit my mom with a darker look than I ever thought I would. "Leave it," I said in a firm tone, a wave of protectiveness washing over me. "Stop controlling everything. It's not your office anymore."

At that, Mom looked at me, holding my gaze for a long moment. She finished her tea, set the teacup back in the saucer with expert precision, and dabbed at her mouth with a cloth napkin. "I'll see you tomorrow, darling. With Mallory."

"You will," I said tightly. "Can't wait."

THE TIE AROUND MY NECK WAS ITCHY.

I wore them every day for work, but tonight's tie seemed tighter than ever. It felt as though it was trying to strangle me, but that was just my mother in my head. She basically had a summer house there, and I shuddered as the sleek black car she'd hired to take us to the mixer pulled up outside Mallory's house.

It was beautiful. The realtor in me couldn't help but

admire the perfect white trimmings of the windows and doors and the matching garage door. The drive and path to the front door were a lovely gray paving that matched perfectly to the white and gray stone façade of the house.

Flowers adorned the yard in the front, and I got out of the car immediately enjoying the scent of the late summer blooms.

Adjusting my tie one more time, I knocked on the door three times and stepped back.

The door swung open, revealing a short woman with gray hair pulled back into a bun. Her beady eyes explored every inch of me until she sniffed and said through bright pink lips, "Who the damn are you?"

Well, shit. Was this the aunt? Or was she an associate of the President? Because that's how she was looking at me—like she was a secret service agent or something.

"Cameron Reid, ma'am. I'm Mallory's boss." I held my hand out for her to shake, but she ignored it, so I dropped it down like a scolded child.

She leaned forward, narrowing her eyes even more. "You look too young to be a boss. How old are you?"

"Twenty-eight."

"Are you single?"

I swallowed. "Yes, ma'am, I am."

"Why?"

"I'm sorry?"

She straightened up and smacked her lips. "You're young. You're rich. You're handsome. What's wrong with you?"

"Aunt Grace." A woman who held a remarkable resemblance to Mallory appeared over the older woman's shoulder and rested her hands on her upper arms. "Why don't you go and sit down in the living room? The poor young man doesn't want to be interrogated on the doorstep."

"I was just seeing if he was boyfriend material."

"Yes. The entire neighborhood heard you. Go inside." She physically turned the old woman around and directed her into another room before coming back to me. She smiled, and I noted that her eyes were the exact same shade as Mallory's. "I'm so sorry," she said, clasping her hands to her chest.

I smiled. "It's fine. Cameron Reid. Mallory's boss." I held my hand out to her, and she took it, giving it a firm shake.

"Helen Harper, Mallory's mom. She's just finishing up now. Would you like to come in and wait?"

I hesitated.

"Don't worry. My aunt will be off sulking somewhere now that I've told her off."

I cracked a smile. "Sure." I followed her inside the house, admiring the minimalistic décor of the hallway. It was all done in cream, and I paused until I realized the floor was wooden, not carpet. "Would you like me to take off my shoes, Mrs. Harper?"

"Honey, call me Helen. And you keep those shoes on—she'll only be a minute." She beamed at me. "Would you like a drink while you wait?"

"I'm fine, thank you." I tugged at my tie again and loosened it just a little.

The old lady shuffled into the kitchen, clasping an empty whiskey glass. She eyed me before she grabbed a whiskey bottle from the counter and poured a generous helping of it.

Then, without a word, she left again.

Helen stared at her retreating back and winced as she looked at me. "I'm so sorry about her. She's incredibly grumpy today."

"It's fine. My grandma was the same. Whiskey and cigarettes and that was her sorted." I shrugged. "She drank a bottle a week and smoked a pack a day, and the woman was never sick."

"Huh. Maybe I should take away the whiskey and see if the cigarettes finish her off," she muttered, grabbing her own glass. She sipped. "Sorry. It's a rough week."

"Don't worry about it. If I had to live with my elderly relatives, I'd drink, too." I grinned and leaned against the table.

She tipped the glass toward me. "I like you. If you weren't her boss, I'd take you as a son-in-law."

"Mom!"

I burst out laughing as Helen winked at me. "She's fine. You should have heard what your aunt was saying." I turned to look at Mallory and paused.

Holy shit.

Her dark hair fell around her shoulders in loose curls. Her blue eyes seemed brighter than usual, thanks to the dark colors that were swept over her eyelids, and her full lips were painted a bright shade of red that perfectly matched her dress.

A dress that hugged her body from her breasts to her knees, revealing curves I didn't know she had.

I knew she was beautiful, but right now, she was downright sexy.

And a part of me wanted to rip the dress right off her.

"I don't want to know," she said, fiddling with a button on her blazer. She peered up through long eyelashes, pausing when she saw me looking at her. "Hi." Her voice was a little squeakier than normal. "Do I look okay? Your mom was vague on the details, and honestly, I was too busy wondering how not to fall over in my heels when you told me. If it's too much, I can go change or—"

I smiled slowly. "You look beautiful. It's perfect."

"Oh." Shock flashed in her eyes. Her cheeks turned a

rosy shade of pink as she briefly dropped her eyes. "Thank you."

Her mom watched the entire exchange with a smile from behind her glass—one that quickly dropped as an elderly man joined us in the kitchen.

He looked over Mallory before turning to me. "Who are you and why are you giving my granddaughter bedroom eyes?"

"Dad!" Helen gasped.

"And that's our cue," Mallory said, reaching for me. She grabbed my arm and tugged, dragging me toward the front door. "Bye, Mom, Grandad, see ya, bye, don't wait up!"

She literally yanked me through the door and slammed it behind us. Her sigh was heavy, and she met my eyes with a resigned look. "I am so sorry."

"Don't worry about it." I touched her arm. "I was totally giving you bedroom eyes for a second there."

Her jaw dropped.

Laughing, I touched her back and guided her to the car. "Come on. Let's go before we're late and Mom loses her mind at me."

"You were giving me bedroom eyes?" She stared at me.

I stopped us a few feet from the car. "Eyes on where you're walking. I watched you trip on the rug this morning. I don't want to be responsible for you breaking your ankle in those heels."

She shoved me in the arm with a half-smile. "I was focusing on not spilling your coffee."

"True." I released her to open the car door. "And somehow, you managed not to."

"Exactly. Give me some credit." She grinned and got into the car.

I closed the door behind her then walked around to the other side and got in myself. "Let's go, shall we?"

THIRTEEN

MALLORY

I WAS NOT CUT OUT FOR THIS.

That much was painstakingly obvious.

I hadn't even stepped foot in the vast, wooden double doors that were apparently the entrance to this huge-ass house, and I already knew I'd stick out like a sore thumb.

Agreeing to this was a mistake.

That didn't even take into account that this little adventure had started off as a total nightmare. First with Aunt Grace answering the door—I still had no desire to learn what she'd said—then my mom, then Grandpa, and Cameron himself admitting he'd given me bedroom eyes.

I was fairly sure he'd been teasing me, but he had given me a long, good look when he'd turned around. It wasn't like I was an expert at flirting. I always looked a little out of my depth when I actually tried, and that included eyeing people up.

Jade once told me I looked like I was plotting a guy's murder, and unless you're a serial killer, it's probably not that sexy.

So maybe Cameron had been giving me bedroom eyes.

That just made this an even worse idea than it already was.

I hesitated as Cameron reached for the door. Nerves fluttered in my stomach, mostly because I wasn't sure I was ready to meet his parents. At least, not in a formal setting like this.

Why couldn't they have popped into the office where I could have escaped?

"Hey." Cameron stopped with his hand on the door. "You'll be fine. I promise I won't leave you alone all night."

I wasn't sure that was a good idea, either. "I don't know enough about real estate to be of any use here at all."

"Look." He released the door and stepped toward me. "Don't worry about that. I'll refer to you as my new assistant all night, and nobody will ask you a thing except how you like working for me."

"And I should probably refrain from mentioning my current list of mishaps."

His eyes glinted with humor. "Not that your affinity for mischief isn't adorable, but yes."

"You think the fact I'm a total klutz is adorable?"

"Yeah, but I also think babies are cute, and they shit and scream, so take that as you will."

"I'm not entirely sure how to respond to that," I said, eyeing the door right before it opened.

I knew instantly the woman in the frame was Cameron's mother. Not only did she have the same, bright blue eyes that he had, but she just looked like she would match the voice on the phone.

I know. It was a weird thing, but that was how I felt about it.

She was tall and slim and looked ten years younger than she had to be. She had dark brown hair that was pulled back into what seemed like an elegant chignon at the base of her neck with a few wisps framing her face.

She pursed dark red lips and turned her attention to Cameron, sliding her hands over her black dress as she did so. "Why are you standing here on the steps? Don't you know I have things for you to do inside?"

"You look beautiful, Mom," he replied, stepping forward to press a kiss to her cheek. "We were just talking about tonight, not delaying anything."

Shrewd blue eyes darted my way. "If I didn't know better, I'd say you were avoiding introducing me to your assistant, especially since the poor woman is still standing there while we talk."

Good God, the woman was intimidating.

Cameron took a deep breath and smiled. "Good thing you know better, huh?" He tossed me a wink and touched a hand to the small of my back, forcing me to take a step toward the woman who, I was almost sure, was of the devil. "Mom, this is my new assistant, Mallory Harper. Mallory, this is my mother, Cordelia Reid."

"It's a pleasure to meet you, Mrs. Reid," I said, extending my hand to her.

She took it, her lips twitching as we shook. "The feeling is mutual, Miss Harper. As I said on the phone, I've heard wonderful things about you."

"Oh, please call me Mallory. Miss Harper is my aunt, and, well…" I shot Cameron a look.

"She's an interesting woman," he said dryly. "Wants to know what's wrong with me because, to quote her loosely, I'm young, rich, and handsome, yet single."

"Yes, well, we're all wondering that, dear," Cordelia said simply and turned to me. "In that case, Mallory, please call me Cordelia."

"Coincidentally," Cameron added, "The conversation with Mallory's aunt was quite uncomfortable. Not unlike this one. Shall we go inside before the neighbors pry?"

Cordelia sniffed. "Yes. That Louise Mayfair across the street is desperate to find out how I keep my roses so alive. I wouldn't put it past her to start a rumor that you're dating."

"It would stop your friends trying to set me up with their daughters," Cameron muttered, touching my back to guide me inside. "And trust me, I've been out with women far worse than Mallory."

Although probably not as much of a hot mess as me, but whatever.

"I didn't mean it in a derogatory way, darling." Cordelia reached back and checked her chignon without looking at us. She led the way like an army captain leading his men to battle. "But I do so hate rumors. Anyway. How is work? Are you keeping busy? Mallory, how are you settling in?"

Wow. So many questions.

I glanced at Cameron.

He half-grinned at me, directing me into the kitchen after his mom. It was freaking huge—the white cupboards all gleamed, and the island housed both a wine rack and some seating for four people. The other end of the kitchen held a huge television on the wall and a large, U-shaped sofa in cream leather. Through a large archway I could see a dining room with a long, rectangular table, and another arch led to what I presumed was the living room.

"Work is good," Cameron said, taking the lead on the conversation. "We booked several viewings today, and Mallory has four new properties to list on the website on Monday. I also think I've decided on the new permanent agent, so downstairs is expanding nicely, too."

She nodded.

Cameron nudged me, and I realized it was my turn to answer the question she'd directed at me.

"Oh—I think it's going well. I've done a lot of admin work before, starting for my dad when I was a teen, so it's more a change of setting than anything. I haven't spent a lot of time with the others, but Cameron's made me feel very welcome."

"As he should. That's his job." She nodded and turned around. "I'm glad you're settling in, darling. It's a gratifying job. That's how I met Cameron's father, you know. I was his assistant."

"No, you didn't." Cameron took a bottle of white wine from an ice bucket. "You knew each other before you worked for him. You only tell the story this way because you think it's more romantic."

She batted her long eyelashes. "Is that a problem?"

"No, but I keep telling you—if you want to fictionalize your love story, write a damn book." He turned his attention to me. "Is Sauvignon Blanc okay?"

I took a deep breath and nodded. I wasn't going to lie, I was incredibly intimidated by Cordelia, but at the same time, I kind of really wanted to be her friend.

She was very prim and proper, almost stereotypical British-like in her mannerisms despite being American, but

I could see that she had a good heart beneath her somewhat cold exterior.

She struck me as the kind of woman who liked things done, but only if they were done her way.

I could relate. I was also partial to having things done my way.

Although that was probably more of a female thing than it is an individual trait…

"Thank you," I managed to eke out when Cameron handed me the glass.

He gave me a smile that made my heart thud. You know the kind—slow and lazy but stupidly sexy.

Or maybe that was the suit. Or both. I didn't know. I did, however, know that I was developing a crush on my boss that I needed to get over pronto.

"Fine, I'll write a book," Cordelia said, accepting her own glass from Cameron. "But I'm still going to tell Mallory all about it."

"I have no doubt," Cameron said dryly.

THERE WERE A LOT OF PEOPLE HERE.

A lot of *wealthy* people. As in, they wore earrings that cost more than my entire outfit, and this red dress was one

I'd splurged on for special occasions.

I'd spent the last ninety minutes attached to Cameron's side. In fact, he'd had one hand on me almost the entire evening, and I hated to admit that his hand on my back or my arm had made me feel a lot better.

He was obviously familiar with these people, and quite honestly, it was just about enough to make me have a good think about this weird little crush I was developing on him.

This was a whole different world.

All I had going for me at this point was the fact I hadn't yet tripped over my own feet, spilled a drink, or walked into anyone.

Mind you, the drink thing was probably because Cameron was firmly in control of pouring wine, and he was only filling my glass halfway. That probably had something to do with the fact that it was the 'proper' way to drink wine, but I'd never taken much stock with that.

In fact, wine was about the only liquid I'd never spilled. Alcohol in general, actually.

Coffee? Sure. Water? Always. Juice? Quite regularly.

Alcohol? The nectar of the Gods? Hell to the no.

I smiled as a couple whose names I'd already forgotten left us in peace. Cameron melted us back into the corner of the living room and once again pressed his hand to my back, leaning down.

His mouth was so close to my ear that I could feel his

breath skitter across my skin. "How are you feeling?"

"Like I'm not really a fancy mixer type of person," I said slowly. "I'd go for Chex Mix over hors-d'oeuvres."

"Me, too. Chex Mix, popcorn, chips and salsa..." He shrugged one shoulder. "I don't go for these parties either, but my mother loves them."

It was true enough. Cordelia had been holding court all evening so far, the absolute epitome of a perfect hostess. She'd hired servers who mingled with champagne on trays and those fucky little snacks I'd been avoiding.

I'd heard there was dessert, and I was holding out.

"How does she do it?" I asked Cameron, leaning into him a little. "She actually enjoys being around people, doesn't she?"

He chuckled, dropping his chin. "She does. She's extremely sociable. She thrives on being around other people, especially when they're as driven and formidable as she is."

"Formidable. That's one word for her."

"I feel like she and your aunt would get along."

I shuddered. "Don't. Did she really ask you what was wrong with you?"

He nodded, shoulders shaking with laughter. "She did. She asked me why I was single, and when I said I didn't understand, she said that I was young, rich, and handsome, then asked what was wrong with me. Luckily, your mom saved me at that point."

"And proceeded to tell you she'd accept you as a son-in-law."

"Yeah, but only because I approved of her drinking."

"That will do it," I mused. "It's kind of tense right now. We don't all get along often because we all have quite strong personalities. At least on my mom's side. My dad pretty much just sits there and lets us all get on with it."

"Like mine?" He laughed, nodding toward where his dad was standing to the side of his mom, nursing a whiskey, watching the world go by.

I giggled behind my hand. His dad was everything his mom wasn't—quiet, sweet, and wrapped me in a big bear hug the second he'd laid eyes on me. But I sensed he had a tough interior that meant he would slaughter anyone who dared cross him or his family.

In a weird way, they were like yin and yang, fitting perfectly together.

It was apparent now as we watched them. She held everyone's attention, telling an exciting story that included hand movements and raucous laughter from her group. He stood beside her, smiling and watching her with what could only be described as pure love.

It reminded me a lot of my parents.

A shiver ran down my spine, and I looked toward Cameron. He'd been watching me watch them, and I cocked my head as if to ask what he was looking at, but all he did was smile, shrug, and turn toward the young woman walking toward us.

She was beelining for him.

"Oh no," he muttered.

"What?"

I swear, his hand crept an inch closer to my hip, almost as if he was gripping tighter to me.

"Cameron!" She stepped up and air-kissed him, despite his reluctance to return the gesture.

I wasn't shocked that she was tall and blonde and incredibly pretty.

Weren't all the thorns in your side tall, blonde, and beautiful?

She touched a hand to his arm, leaning in flirtatiously. "How are you?"

"I'm well, thank you, Rachel. Have you met my new assistant, Mallory?"

She flicked a baby-blue gaze my way. "No."

Charming.

"I've been trying to call you," she said, stepping a little closer.

Cameron responded by taking a step back. I wanted to tell him that wasn't a good idea because we were in a corner, and there was a big-ass wall behind us that would stop his escape.

"I couldn't get through," Rachel continued, flicking her hair. "Did you get a new number?"

I glanced up at Cameron. He looked like he wanted to be anywhere but in that corner with her, and an idea flashed through my mind.

I held my small clutch against my body. "Excuse me, my phone is ringing. Cameron, could you hold this while I take this call?" I shoved my wine glass at him, barely giving him time to answer.

I walked away, making a big show of diving into my purse for my phone. It caught the attention of Cordelia who looked at Cameron and Rachel and then me, frowning. I waved my phone at her, making sure to show her the back, and smiled.

As soon as she turned her attention back to them, I slipped into the spacious back yard and away from a large group of expensively-dressed people to fake my call.

Plastering concern on my face, I nodded, making several 'mm-ing' noises and acting as though there was an emergency on the end of the line.

I could feel eyes on me from inside, so I held the phone to my collarbone as if I were protecting the call and slipped back inside. Cordelia's eyes followed me the entire way as I sidled up to Cameron.

Rachel was even closer to him than she had been when I'd left, and I had to stifle a smile as I touched his arm.

"Excuse me for interrupting," I said, looking between them both, absolutely not sorry at all. "Cameron, Amanda just called about a problem with a listing she needs to put up on Monday. Do you have a minute to speak to her?"

"Now?" He checked his watch. "Isn't it a little late?"

"She said earlier she was taking some work home to get ahead. She's on the line." I pointed at my phone and grimaced.

He stared at me for a second. "Sure. Rachel—sorry. Have to handle this."

He touched my upper back and guided me out into the hallway, then into another room and shut the door. Bookcases lined the wall to my left, and a desk with an expensive-looking computer was at the far end, framed by windows that looked out onto beautifully manicured gardens.

"Mom's study," he said, obviously seeing my confusion. "Pass the phone."

I was still holding it to my collarbone. "Oh." I pulled it away and looked at it before showing him the screen. "No, it's fine. She didn't call." I shrugged.

"What?" He froze, staring at me, a frown creasing his brow. "What do you mean, she didn't call?"

I shrugged again. "You looked like you wanted to be anywhere but with Rachel, so I faked the call to get you away."

Cameron stared at me for a long moment. "You're a genius."

"Please, I'm a woman. Do you know how many phone calls I've faked to get Jade away from a guy who was hitting on her?" I rolled my eyes. "It's literally part of the playbook. Also, you're welcome."

He laughed, running his hand through his hair. "Thank you. Seriously. She's been trying to get me on a date for two years now, but I'm not interested."

"Well, we just have to wait long enough to make it believable." I sank into one of the stylish, cream leather chairs that sat close to the desk. "Five minutes or so. Your mom saw me on the phone, so she won't be suspicious."

"Were you a spy in another life?"

"No. Like I said: I'm a woman. I'm used to being the wingman who gets rid of unwanted advances." I smirked. "Also, thanks for bringing my wine."

He laughed and handed it to me before sitting in the chair opposite me. "You're welcome. Consider that my thank you."

"A raise would work."

"You've worked there a week. Settle down."

"It was worth a shot." I grinned. "Well, I'm here for you. Appointments, phone calls, house listings, and unwanted advances."

He barked a laugh, flattening his hand against his

stomach. "I'll keep that in mind."

I winked, probably looking like a sloth with a twitch, and sipped my wine. We sat together in silence for a good couple of minutes, and that allowed me to look around the room.

And at Cameron.

All right, mostly at Cameron.

His suit fit him to perfection. I should have expected it, of course. I was used to him wearing one, but his choice was usually gray. Gray pants, gray jacket, white shirt, black tie. He'd changed it up tonight, wearing a black suit that was closer to a tuxedo than your everyday suit.

His deep blue tie was the only thing that stopped him looking like he was headed to a wedding.

It suited him. Almost more than the gray. Maybe it was the lines the black jacket gave his upper body, the complete illusion of the shape of his torso. I knew without seeing them that his body was packed with muscle. You didn't have to have X-ray vision to see that the man was blessed in every way possible.

Well. Not every way. I hadn't—yeah. I wasn't going down that route.

I broke my stare of him, a spark of fear rocketing through me that he'd notice. The last thing I wanted was for him to realize I'd been checking him out.

Ugh.

But it was so unfair.

I wanted to check him out like a library book.

His dark hair, his hot stubble, his perfect lips, his beautiful blue eyes…

Well, even library books had a time limit. I guessed this was mine, and I wasn't willing to take on any kind of fine for my staring.

He opened his mouth to say something, but the door to the study opened. Both of us shot up to sit bolt upright, our gazes darting toward it.

It was Cordelia.

She stepped inside, pursing her lips.

"It's my fault," I said quickly, standing up.

She held up one hand. "Cameron, your father is sharing a tipple with Leonard Fortune. He'd like you to be there to discuss the potential for a Denver office."

I swallowed. Hard. That sounded like I was in trouble.

Cameron flashed me a glance before he stood, finishing his wine and putting the empty glass on the desk. "Of course, Mom. Are they in his office?"

She nodded. "Take a decanter of scotch, won't you? They're both in an excellent mood, and I daresay a little more of that won't hurt."

"No problem at all." He flashed me one more concerned look before he left the study, shutting the door behind him.

Leaving me with his mom.

Alone.

"Mrs. Reid, I—"

"Cordelia," she interrupted. Then, she sighed. "Goodness, it's exhausting, isn't it? Pretending you like people."

Shocked, I stared at her as she tugged at the stomach of her dress and filled the seat Cameron had just vacated.

She looked up at me. "Mallory, darling, do sit down. You're making the room look untidy."

I sat down so fast I hurt my ass.

She tittered a laugh, but there was nothing insincere about it. "I know. I've been sociable all evening, but even I reach a point where I need to check out." She crossed one leg over the other and cradled her wine glass in one hand.

Her eyes were incredible. They made you feel both comfortable and completely out of your depth with one look.

If I could grow up to be anyone...

"Tell me, darling. What was the phone call so important that you had to drag Cameron away from the get-together?"

I could lie. The option was there. She didn't know. It could have been anything—but nothing that would lead me to have an explanation as to why we'd been sitting and chatting like old friends in here.

Besides, I was sure she knew.

She'd looked at Rachel like she was a bad rash on a good day, and that was all I needed to tell the truth.

"He was uncomfortable around Rachel." I met her eyes. "I saw an opportunity to get him out of the situation, and I took it."

Cordelia stared at me for a long moment. Then, she downed her wine.

I was expecting...

Well, I didn't know what I was expecting.

Cameron might have been the boss, but it was clear who pulled strings in the company. If Cordelia didn't like me, there was no doubt I'd be out of a job on Monday morning.

I didn't expect her to get up, open a desk drawer, and pull out a half-sized bottle of Sauvignon.

"Another?" she asked, holding up the bottle.

I'd only had two.

I did as she did and finished my wine so I could hand her an empty glass.

"Excellent choice. It's a wonderful wine, from Southern France." She opened the bottle and removed the cork with a finesse I could only dream of, then poured us two glasses.

Proper glasses.

"I don't know what I like more," I said. "The ease you pulled the cork with, or how you actually like your wine."

She set down the bottle and, with a smirk firmly on her face, picked up her glass. "Cheers to that."

We clinked glasses, and she was right. It was a delicious wine, and that was just enough for me to ignore the fact I was sitting here with my boss' mother, drinking wine, hiding away from everyone.

"You," she said after a moment. "Are perhaps one of the smartest people in that room."

I raised my eyebrows.

"You recognized the situation for what it was. Rachel Cooper is a nightmare of the highest degree," Cordelia continued, her steady gaze holding mine. "She's been desperate to date my son for a long time now, despite his assurances otherwise."

"Despite him telling her where to go, you mean."

"Well, yes." Her lips twitched. "I recognized what you did immediately. Like I said—you're incredibly smart, Mallory, and I like you. You could go far in this industry, and I don't just mean as my husband's assistant. I've watched you network tonight, and to someone who didn't know you were nervous, you've handled it like a pro."

I swallowed and sipped. "Thank you."

"You won't deny you were nervous?"

"No offense, but have you ever met yourself?"

She laughed, dropping her head back. "I suppose I can be quite overbearing."

"Quite overbearing? You strong-armed me into this. If I weren't here, I'd be at home watching Netflix with no pants on and eating my body weight in ice-cream."

Another laugh escaped her. "Well, I wanted to meet you. What can I say?" The smile that lit up her face was different than the others—there was a warm tone to it that made me smile, too.

She took a long drink of her wine until it was at a similar level to what it was when she came in here, then she took one more sip.

I couldn't help but smile.

"Time to get back to it." She smiled at me, a genuinely warm smile that reached her eyes and made them shine, and walked to the door.

There, she stopped.

Slowly, she turned, making eye contact with me. "Mallory?"

"Yes?"

"I don't recommend wearing a dress like that to work. My son is easily distracted." Her lips twitched once, giving the slightest illusion of a smile, but it was the glint in her eye that made me blush.

With that, she left, making sure the door clicked behind her.

Hooooo-ey.

I was in trouble.

FOURTEEN

MALLORY

"ALL RIGHT?" THE VOICE IN MY EAR WAS LOW AND BREATHY, AND I jumped.

I'd not long gotten whisked into a conversation with Cordelia and her friends that'd lasted far too long for my liking. Not to mention I hadn't been able to offer anything until one of the women had mentioned being after a lodge in the mountains.

Then, I'd been everyone's best friend. I'd avoided the Broughton Lodge, knowing that Cynthia wanted it—and she happened to be present—but I offered inside information on the one I knew I was listing on Monday.

Cordelia had just about burst with happiness.

Now, I was alone, and it was Cameron who'd snuck up behind me and whispered in my ear.

I nodded. "Your mom corralled me for a while, but I think one of her friends are going to call about that new lodge first thing on Monday?"

"See?" He slid beside me, one hand touching my back. "And you thought you'd hate this all."

"Oh, I didn't say I liked it."

He laughed, stepping into me. "Ready for a break?"

I nodded, and he guided me out of the back door to a decking a little further away from the house. It was set high up in the town, and the decking looked out over the town I called home.

Lights blinked all over, and it was early enough in the year that we could still see the vague outline of the mountains behind it. It was barely there, but it was beautiful all the same.

Solar lights pinged to life as we took to the seating area, but instead of sitting, Cameron went to the fencing that surrounded the area.

I joined him, leaning against it the way he was. "It's so quiet here."

He nodded. "They got the best plot in town, no doubt about it. You wouldn't believe there was an entire neighborhood here."

"Nope. It's amazing. There's so much space."

"Well, it won't surprise you that what Mom wants, Mom gets."

I laughed. "Not at all."

He sighed, twirling the whiskey glass. "You've handled this well, you know. Tonight. All these people. Being out of your depth."

I took a deep breath. "I hope so. Your mom saw what I'd done with Rachel, and she liked it. She doesn't like her."

"Never has. Doesn't stop Rachel trying, though."

"I almost admire that kind of tenacity."

"Don't. I dated her cousin, and she's still trying to date me." He shook his head and sighed before standing up straighter. "My mother usually nips those in the bud, but she's persistent."

"She's persistent all right. Your mom actually thanked me for it."

He laughed, looking over at me. "She likes you. I can't remember the last time she was so nice to someone who was outside her friendship circle."

I wasn't going to tell him what she'd said—or what she'd implied with her comment about my dress.

I loved this dress. I knew it made me look good. And I also knew how he'd looked at me when he'd seen me.

The last thing I wanted was for anything to happen because of this damn dress.

I was going to burn the fucking thing.

"Thank you," Cameron said. He nudged my arm and smiled. "For making this night more bearable than it would have been otherwise."

I clutched my glass a little tighter and met his eyes. God, they were fucking dreamy. "You're welcome. Thank you for making it so that I didn't really have to talk to anyone."

"And you didn't even trip over."

"Yet," I said. "*Yet*. The night is still young."

He dropped his head and laughed, shaking it gently. "It's mostly over now if you want to leave. You don't have to stay here any longer."

"Sounds like you're trying to get rid of me."

Peering over at me, his lips tugged to the side. "No. I was just letting you know that the option was there."

"Well, thank you," I said with a hint of sarcasm. "Are you bundling me into a car and sending me home?"

"No." He chuckled. "I was going to get in the car with you and take you home. My mother would have a fit if I sent you alone. Besides, if I take you home, I don't have to come back."

"Ahh, I knew there was an ulterior motive." I shook my head and tutted. "You're using me to make your grand escape."

"Well, I was trying to hide that part, but since you pushed…"

I rolled my eyes and stood up straight. "It's not enough that I make you coffee and schedule your appointments, is it?"

"You do make good coffee," he mused, straightening up. "Are you ready?"

"If I don't take these shoes off soon, I might just rip off my feet," I admitted. "I rarely wear heels."

"Why? Because you fall over thin air?"

I glared at him as I finished my wine. "Remember who makes your coffee. Carry on, and I'm going to start making it with salt."

Cameron shuddered and took the empty glass from me. We made our way back inside, where he handed the glasses to a server with an empty tray and touched my back again. "Can you see my parents? We should say goodbye before we go."

I scanned the room. "She's in the middle of a conversation in the living room, but your dad is standing by the fireplace."

Almost as if I'd summoned him, Cameron's dad turned and looked at us, nodded once, and started walking toward us.

"Leaving now?" he asked, smiling warmly.

"Yeah. We don't want to interrupt Mom, so can you tell her we said goodbye?" Cameron asked.

He nodded. "Of course. Mallory, it was lovely to meet you." He leaned forward and kissed my cheek.

I smiled. "You, too. Thank you for having me here tonight."

"My pleasure."

We waved and left, and I took a deep breath as soon as the car engine rumbled to life.

Cameron laughed next to me. "I'm glad I'm not the only one who feels like that whenever I leave their house."

I looked over at him. "I don't mean it like that. More like, I can finally sit down without wondering if I'm being stared at, and I don't have to worry about hiding the fact I'm a klutz."

"You worry about hiding that?"

"Would you have hired me if you'd known before that I would one, step out in front of your car because I was daydreaming; two, spill coffee all over your desk; and three, send my work flying across the floor because I can't shut a window?"

He raised his eyebrows. "Well, first, the window wasn't your fault. Mostly."

"Mostly."

"And we all spill coffee."

"And the car?"

"I got nothing, Mallory. Most sane people don't walk out in front of cars."

"But would it have stopped you hiring me?"

He paused. "It would have made me hesitate. For what it's worth, I'm glad I didn't know any of that. I like working with you."

I smiled and pushed some hair behind my ear.

"When you're not spilling coffee all over my desk."

I dropped the smile.

He stared at me for a minute before bursting into laughter. I wanted to stay mad, but his laugh was so infectious, that all it took was one small nudge from him and I was laughing along with him.

The ride to my house didn't take long, and we took the rest of it in silence. It was a comfortable one, and through it, my mind started to wander.

Not far. Just to what he looked like under that white shirt, but never mind.

The car pulled up outside my house. The porch light clicked on, illuminating my mom's flowerbeds, and I swear I saw a curtain twitch.

It wasn't that late, but Dad had mentioned taking Mom out for drinks, so I assumed they were out doing whatever it was fifty-something-year-old people did in bars.

I wouldn't know. I didn't hang out with my parents in bars.

That left Great Aunt Grace and Grandpa. Grandpa would have already put his ornery ass in bed, but I had no doubt that Aunt Grace was up waiting for me to come home so she could snoop.

Cameron opened my car door for me and offered his hand. I took it, stepping out, with my clutch held tight to my stomach. The wind had picked up while we'd been at his parents'. My stomach fluttered as our eyes briefly met, and I ducked my head to get rid of the feeling.

Boss, Mallory. He's your damn boss.

My hormones needed to settle their tea kettle.

Cameron shut the door behind me and walked me to the front door. The curtains definitely twitched, and if he saw it, he was smart enough not to mention it.

We stopped on the doorstep and turned to each other. It felt like the ending to a date in a flirty movie—you know, the guy walks the girl to the door, they thank each other for the night, then he leans in, kisses her slowly, hand in her hair…

I swallowed and took a step back from Cameron. "Thank you for bringing me home."

He smiled. "My pleasure. Thank you for coming tonight, even though you really didn't want to."

"Well, I didn't have much of a choice."

"I know. But still."

I looked up at him as a gust of wind circled us, taking my hair with it. I made a squeaking noise as my hair whipped around my face, blowing into my mouth and over my eyes.

Cameron laughed, and the next thing I knew, he was standing right in front of me, and his fingers were on my skin.

His fingertips brushed across my forehead and down my cheek, brushing the hair away from my eyes. It was a feather-light touch, yet it burned me. I was hyperaware of him, of every curve and line of his face, of how the pad of his finger was dangerously soft as it glided to tuck my hair behind my ear.

With a dry mouth, I forced myself to swallow the best I could.

His eyes were bright and wide, but there was a slight shadow in them, like he was holding something back.

I was holding something back.

My lips.

I wanted to kiss his goddamn face off.

But I didn't.

Not even when he dropped his gaze to my lips for a fleeting second. In fact, the look was so short I may have even imagined it.

Until he did it again.

I definitely didn't imagine it.

My boss was looking at my lips like he wanted to kiss them.

Abort. Mission.

I cleared my throat and stepped back, slicing through the tension. He did the exact same thing, except he went down the step onto the path. We stared awkwardly at each other for a moment.

Cameron coughed and rubbed the back of his neck. "I'll see you Monday morning?"

"Afternoon," I corrected him. "You have viewings all morning."

"Crap."

"I'll check the diary and email them to you tomorrow."

He grinned. "Thanks. You're the best."

"Yeah, well, I won't put salt in your coffee just yet." I smiled, gripping hold of the door handle. "See you Monday."

He winked and turned back to the car, leaving me to push open the front door and, blissfully, enter a silence house.

Thank God for that.

FIFTEEN

MALLORY

MY PHONE WAS RINGING INCESSANTLY.

I gripped the towel around my body tightly and ran across the house, trying to stop my towel turban from falling in the process of making it to my room. The ringing stopped, only to immediately start up again.

"Goddamn it, who's calling me at this stupid hour?"

It was seven-thirty in the morning. The only phone call I wanted at seven-thirty was Cameron telling me I could have a day off.

As luck would have it, the name on the screen was Cameron, but given how enthusiastically he was calling me, it wasn't to give me a day off.

"Hello?"

"Mallory! I'm in trouble."

"Oh, God. Do I need to bail you out of jail?"

"What?" He laughed. "No, but good to know you're willing, should the need ever arise."

I slumped onto my bed. "What's the problem?"

"My grandfather wants to look at some properties this afternoon. I don't have time to go to the office to get the information on the houses he wants to see. Can you do me a huge favor and run by the office and bring them to my house?" He rushed the words out. "I'm running stupidly fucking late because my alarm didn't go off, and I'm basically going property to property today."

"Uh… Okay. When do you need them?"

"In the next thirty minutes."

I looked down at my wet, towel-clad body. "All right, but I should warn you that I just got out of the shower, and the fanciest thing I'm going to be wearing is yoga pants."

"You're good. It's fine. Go into the office late. Can you do it?"

I made a noise that sounded vaguely like a starving raccoon before ultimately giving in. "Text me your address."

"You're the best ever, and I owe you dinner. I'll send it right now. I'll leave the front door unlocked for you. Gotta go." He hung up before I could say goodbye.

I guess I was wearing yoga pants this morning.

I quickly set to getting ready, stopping long enough

only to pull my thick hair into a braid and do something with the mess that were my eyebrows.

Oh, and lipstick.

Just because you were wearing yoga pants and had wet hair didn't mean a lick of lipstick wouldn't make your day brighter.

I hurried into the kitchen. "Hey, Mom, I need to get some info from the office and take it to Cameron at home. Can I borrow your car?"

She looked up from her plate of French toast. "Don't you want breakfast?"

"Emergency," I said. "Save me some?"

Mom nodded. "My keys are in the bowl. I'm meeting Sandra and Kate at ten for coffee—will you be long?"

"Nope. I'll be back in less than an hour. Thanks!" I blew her a kiss and snatched her keys from the bowl, then headed out to her little Ford.

I climbed in and made my way to the office. It was freaky being here before eight when Main Street was all but dead. Mostly because I was able to get a parking spot right in front of the building, which was weird in itself.

I pulled up the key. Cameron's text also detailed what information he wanted for his grandfather's showings so I knew exactly where to find it. It didn't take me long to get up to his office and find the folder labeled, "Grandpa."

Snatching it up, I headed back out, locking the door

behind me, and plugged Cameron's address into the GPS built into the dashboard. It showed a ten-minute drive, so I set the folder down on the passenger seat and pulled away.

The drive out to Cameron's house was pleasant and quiet. I didn't get stuck in any traffic, and I ventured into a side of town I was relatively unfamiliar with.

The houses were big and beautiful, stinking of money I didn't have and never would have. The yards were perfectly trimmed and landscaped, completely beautiful and dreamy.

Weird to describe one as dreamy, I know, but whatever.

I pulled up on the curb in front of Cameron's house. It was less landscaped than the others around, and I was also pleasantly surprised to see that it was a little smaller than the others around.

I parked and pulled the keys, slipping the folder up against my stomach as I got out of the car. I locked it, although I probably didn't need to in this neighborhood, and headed for the front door.

Even though he said he'd left it unlocked, it didn't feel right for me to just barge in there like it was nothing. I hesitated on the front step, staring at the dark blue front door inside of me.

The last time I'd seen him, I'd wanted to kiss him.

This wasn't going to be awkward at all.

At least I had the winning combination of lipstick and yoga pants. That was all a girl really needed to be successful in life.

Lipstick. And yoga pants.

I knocked three times and pushed the door open. "It's Mallory. I have the info you wanted," I called, hovering in the hallway. There was no answer, so I shut the door behind me and called out his name.

Nothing.

Hesitantly, I moved through into the rooms. I walked through a tastefully decorated living room in blue and gray, then peeked into a home office that was about as tidy as his actual office.

Not at all, to be honest. And that was after I'd inadvertently made him tidy his desk thanks to a rogue cup of coffee and a coaster.

I left the office before I had the urge to tidy it and moved into a sleek, black kitchen.

Jesus, this place was every inch the bachelor pad, wasn't it? Would I stumble upon a Christian Grey-esque red room on my way through the property?

I took a breath and turned.

And found Cameron.

My boss.

In front of the fridge.

Wearing nothing but a white towel around his waist.

Giving me a damn good view of his body. There were abs for days, at least fifty of them, and about ten pecs.

Mind you, that could have been my view as I panicked about the fact my boss was basically naked in front of me.

I shrieked, jumping back and turning around, almost tossing myself into a door as I did so. "Oh my God. I'm sorry."

There was a breathy chuckle from behind me. "Sorry. I didn't know you'd be here this quickly."

"You told me it was an emergency," I said to the door in front of me. "So I hurried."

"Yeah. Your odd socks give you away."

"Huh?"

"One is neon yellow and the other is pink."

I looked down. "Shit."

Cameron laughed. "Come on. Turn around. I promise I won't let the towel drop."

"I don't—maybe that's not a good idea."

"Mallory, all you have to do is turn around and give me the folder, and then you can run out of here. You're wearing sneakers. You can do that. And probably trip over your own feet."

"Shut up!" I turned around to look at him and froze. He'd won.

He was such a shit.

Cameron grinned, leaning forward, clutching the towel at his hip. "Sorry. Drop the info on the island, and I'll take a look before I go to his house. He'll want to comb over them all anyway. Then you can go and take your embarrassment with you."

"I'm not embarrassed!" I said right as my cheeks turned a flattering shade of bright red. "I'm just shocked!"

"Uh-huh." Cameron took the folder from me and put it on the island. "By the way, Mallory, my face is a few inches higher. As much as I'm sure my belly button would like to hear what you have to say."

I swallowed hard and snapped my gaze up. It wasn't my fault. He was standing in front of me in his kitchen looking like a fucking walking wet dream, and he was calling me out for looking at his abs? Not to mention that goddamn highway to heaven that curved over his hips and dipped down under his towel.

"You—you shut up!" I retorted, jabbing my keys at him. "I'm going to get ready to work, and I don't want to listen to this nonsense about me talking to your belly button!"

"Eyes are up here."

"Put some damn clothes on!" I snapped, turning on my heel and walking back into through the office and the living room.

The sound of Cameron's laughter reached me as I got to the hall and yanked open the front door.

"Bye!" I yelled, slamming it behind me and running down the path to my mom's car.

It was only when I'd securely locked myself inside the vehicle that I took a deep breath.

I'd basically seen my boss naked. Little white towels were the things that dreams were made of, and I swear to God my dream had just fucking well come true right there and then.

A tall, dark, handsome man, wearing nothing but a white towel with abs for days and biceps that would make a rock weep.

Jesus.

I banged my head against the steering wheel three times. The third time, I hit the fucking horn and made it blare out, and a front door opening made me jam the key in the ignition and make the car come to life.

I pulled away from Cameron's house, quickly making the journey back to my house, leaving behind the memory of my hot as hell boss.

In theory.

Not many red-blooded single women could let go of that idea in their head. I was both red-blooded and very, very single, so I couldn't.

I was so single that my vagina had pretty much sewn itself up in anticipation of never getting laid again.

My heart thumped, and I swear I was still blushing as I pulled up on my driveway. The image of Cameron in the towel was firmly stuck in my head. My clitoris was basically crying that I'd left him there looking like a wet dream.

How was I ever going to face him again?

I'd have to quit my job. That was it. The only way to fix this was to quit and never see him ever, ever, ever again.

Slightly dramatic, but I did have a flair for it.

I sat in the car and pulled up my phone.

Me: What do you do when you see your hot boss in a towel?

Jade's response was immediate like I knew it would be.

Jade: U share it with ur best friend. Duh.

Me: Slightly creepy.

Jade: Why? Did u see Cameron naked?

Me: Took some files he wanted to his house and he was in a towel.

Jade: Was he still wet?

Me: Texting you was a mistake.

I sighed and rested my head on the steering wheel again. I should have known she wouldn't have anything constructive to say or actually help me. I was crushing on Cameron Reid big time, and now I had to look him in the eye and hope I didn't see his abs when I did so.

Right.

Now every time I thought of him it wouldn't be of him in a gray suit.

It would be half-naked, in front of the fridge, in a towel.

I was so screwed.

"SO HE DIDN'T COME INTO THE OFFICE? ALL DAY?" JADE NURSED HER frozen margarita like it was a baby.

I shook my head, pulling my mango one toward me. She'd realized I was in trouble for real and dragged me to our favorite Mexican restaurant to talk over the fact I fancied my boss.

"Nope. But he did have a packed day, and he wasn't supposed to come in this morning anyway." I stirred my drink with the straw. "Honestly, I'm glad he didn't come in. I don't think I can look him in the eye ever again."

"It can't be that bad." She dipped a chip in salsa. "It's not like you're a virgin and you've never seen a man before."

"It's been two years. I may as well be a virgin," I grumbled.

"Two years? Ouch. We need to get you laid before your vagina drags you across your office and clamps onto his penis."

"I don't think that's going to happen." But just to be sure, I had to start wearing pants to work. "I need help to deal with this, Jade. You're the people person in this friendship. Help me."

"All right, all right." She held up her hands. "As your best friend, I'll sleep with him instead."

"And people say I'm the problematic one."

She rolled her eyes as our food was brought over. She had quesadilla; I had nachos. "Okay, listen. There's nothing you can do, Mal. You have to suck it up. It's not like you saw him in secret, is it? He knows, and from what you said, he didn't seem to be bothered by it at all."

"No. He was laughing at me," I muttered, focusing on my food. "I don't get it. Like, he didn't care that I was there and basically looking at him naked. I wanted to die."

"Yeah, but you're easily embarrassed." Jade shrugged one shoulder. "A hairless cat would embarrass you."

"Funny."

"It's just part of being Mallory. This stuff just happens to you. Look at all the random, embarrassing things that happen whenever you're around."

As if on cue, like she'd put the challenge out to the universe, the entire restaurant quietened as a guy several tables over got down on one knee.

"Really? A Mexican restaurant?" Jade said under her breath, gaining herself a nod of approval from the girl on the table next to ours.

The air was thick with tension, and not because she was taking ages to answer.

"Uh-oh," I whispered as she got up and walked away.

"Ouch," Jade whispered in return.

The guy stood up awkwardly, still holding the ring box, and after a quick look around, went after her, and the noise in the restaurant returned to normal.

"That was not my fault," I said quickly, dipping a chip in sour cream. "You can't even blame that on me."

"No, but you're a magnet for disaster. You know that."

"I know. That's why I've never had a successful relationship, have to live with my parents, and every job I've ever had I've been let go from because the business has shut down." I sighed, piling sour cream and guac onto a chip. "Not to mention all the other things that happen."

"Like almost getting run over by your new boss, spilling coffee over his desk, then seeing him half-naked."

I groaned. "At least I made it through Saturday night like an adult."

"Yeah, but now you're being a baby, so it doesn't really matter."

"Helpful, Jade, thanks."

"You're welcome. Now, here's what you have to do: go into work tomorrow morning, smile, say hello, and ask if he'd like a coffee. Business as usual. It's only a big deal if you make it one."

"Making things a big deal is basically the only skill I have that means anything."

"Well, drama does go hand in hand with being a klutz."

"Exactly. You take that away from me and you leave me with nothing." I grinned. "But you're right. I know that. So I'll go into work tomorrow and act like everything is fine and I don't want to draw patterns on his abs with my tongue."

Jade lifted her margarita. "Cheers to that."

SIXTEEN

CAMERON

THERE WAS NOTHING MORE AWKWARD THAN YOUR ASSISTANT KNOWING
what you look like practically naked.

Mallory had scared the ever-loving shit out of me. When I'd told her I needed those files quick, I hadn't thought she'd be that damn quick. It was basically fifteen minutes from the call to her showing up at my house.

Not to mention I'd only told her I needed them so quickly because she was, well, Mallory. I assumed she'd get delayed by running over a pigeon or something on her way over.

I'd already decided I wasn't going to make a big deal out of it. She likely would, so I'd be the calm one. Really, it wasn't a big deal. It wasn't like I'd been entirely naked or I'd seen her.

If I'd seen her, all bets would have been off. There was no way I'd ever be able to scrub the image of her in a towel or her underwear off my mind.

Hell, they were on my mind already.

It was making work a problem because I was more focused on the brown-haired, red-lipped woman outside my office.

I shook my head to dislodge those thoughts as I entered the building. It was already busy and bustling downstairs, with all the realtors seemingly out on a viewing or here with someone. I waved good morning to Amanda who was on the phone and headed for the stairs.

Mallory would already be here. Hopefully, she was on the phone or something so I could just slip into my office without having to talk to her just yet.

It was delaying the inevitable, sure, but whatever.

I took the last stair and stepped into the room. She was sitting at her desk, typing away on the computer. She'd pulled her dark hair up into a bun on top of her head, and her always-red lips were pursed as she paused, moving one hand to the mouse and clicking.

A white collar peeked out from the top of her navy and blue striped sweater, and I hated that the one thing I noticed about it was that it hugged her body perfectly.

Fuck me dead.

As if she knew I was staring, she turned to look at me.

A smile broke across her face, and her eyes lit up when they landed on me.

"Good morning!" she chirped. "Would you like a cup of coffee?"

What was going on? I wasn't expecting her to drool over me, but I wasn't expecting her to be so super friendly.

She had never been this friendly.

"Good morning," I said, somewhat hesitantly. "I'd love a cup."

"Great. Let me finish up this email, and I'll bring one in for you." That smile was still in place as she turned back to the computer, then paused, looking back at me. "Oh, your grandfather called. The message is on your desk."

"Thanks." I hesitated as she focused on the screen once more.

All righty, then.

I made my way into my office, giving her one last confused glance before I shut the door behind me.

Who was that, and what have they done with Mallory?

I slid into my chair and picked up the note she'd left on my keyboard. Grandpa wanted to take another look at one of the houses we'd seen yesterday, so I scribbled a note to remind me to call the owners and see if I could get that scheduled.

I booted up my computer, and I'd barely had a chance to sign in when the door opened and Mallory came in, a coffee in one hand and a plate with a bag in the other.

"I didn't think you'd get breakfast, so I stopped by the bakery on the way here and got you something to eat," she said, setting them both down on the desk. "And I even made your coffee with sugar."

I stared at her.

Not only was she being extra friendly, but she hadn't tripped once.

"Thank you?" I said, blinking.

"You're welcome." She bounced on the balls of her feet and clasped her hands together in front of her stomach. Another big grin stretched over her face, and she literally skipped out of my office like she was high on sugar.

Maybe she was high on sugar. There was a bag of jelly beans on her desk. Perhaps she'd had them for breakfast, and that was the reason for this super cheerful version of her.

I didn't like it.

Still, I let her go about her business outside being super cheery. She was even like that on the phone when it rang.

She had to be having a sugar rush.

I shook my head and dove into the paperwork I had to do. It took me forever to get through it all, and by the time I had, it was lunchtime.

I shut down the computer and got up after checking the time. Mallory was still at her desk, and she had the phone to her ear while she nodded.

"Absolutely. Don't worry about that. Your appointment with Mr. Reid is booked for Wednesday at two p.m. We'll see you then. Buh-bye." She hung up the phone and sighed, then tapped the appointment into the calendar we shared on the computer.

"Hey," I said. "I'm going out to grab lunch. Do you want me to bring you anything?"

She looked up, that same bright smile on her face. "Nope. I'm all good. I brought something with me today."

Seriously. What was wrong with her?

"All right, then." I tugged on my shirt collar, tapped my pants to make sure I had my wallet with me and left her to it.

She started humming as she clicked around on the computer, and I jerked my head back to look at her. I had no idea what she was singing to, but it fit with this weird, over-friendly demeanor she'd had going on all morning.

"Hey, Mallory?"

"Yep?" She looked up at me.

"I believe I promised you dinner for helping me yesterday."

Something flashed in her eyes. "You do?"

"I do. I owe you dinner. Are you free tonight?"

"I—"

"Great. I'll pick you up at six-thirty." I winked and

turned before she could turn me down.

Look at that. There was a little of my mother in me after all.

I SUCCESSFULLY MANAGED TO AVOID MALLORY FOR THE REST OF THE afternoon thanks to two viewings that took a while for me drive out to.

Now, I was pulling up outside her house, ready to take her to dinner.

I couldn't lie and say that I was doing this out of the goodness of my hearts. I wanted to spend time with her—as inappropriate as I knew that was—and I wanted to address what had happened at my house.

Her extra niceness was obviously so she could avoid talking about it. Her cheeks had been so red when she'd left, and if I were her, I wouldn't want to bring it up either.

I honked my horn so she knew I was here. I waited, tapping my fingers against the steering wheel. The clock was ticking, and she still wasn't coming out. I was half tempted to call her.

The last thing I wanted to do was to go to her front door and get corralled by her family again. I didn't think her grandpa would be best pleased to see me, and her aunt was sure to question me again.

Fuck.

I checked the clock. If she didn't come out in another few minutes, I'd bite the bullet and go to the front door.

Unfortunately, sitting here allowed me to get inside my head, namely to ask myself what the fuck I was thinking. Taking my assistant for dinner was a terrible idea. She was young, beautiful, and if she weren't my assistant, I'd be doing everything I could to get to know her better.

Hell, it looked like that's what I was doing anyway.

It was dangerous. I knew it was how people fell in love, I knew it was how my parents fell in love, but it was a testy line to walk.

What happened if the relationship didn't work? Then what? It wasn't like I could leave my job, and I had no desire to ever fire anyone just because we'd broken up.

Jesus fuck, it was so much easier when Casey was my assistant.

I took a deep breath and checked the clock. Mallory still hadn't come out, so I blew out the breath and pulled the keys from the ignition.

And braced myself for her aunt.

Maybe that was where Mallory got her hurricane tendencies from.

I locked the car and walked up to the front door. There was some shouting from inside, and I hesitated before I knocked. I didn't want to interrupt or get in the middle of any family argument.

Before I could make a choice, the door swung open and I came face-to-face with Mallory.

"Quick," she hissed, pushing me back so I almost tripped down the step. She yanked the door shut and grabbed me, pulling me to the car. "Before she comes out here!"

"Before who comes out?"

"Aunt Grace!" She turned when she got to my car. "Cameron!"

I didn't know what was going on. I was, honestly, completely and utterly confused, but I did as she wanted. I hurried to the car and went to open the door for her, but she shook her head.

"No time! Let's go!" She tugged the door open and was in and belted in before I'd even gotten my door open.

The front door of her house opened, and I slipped into the car before anything could happen.

Mallory released a deep breath as I drove away from the car. "Thank you."

"What the hell was all that?"

She adjusted her purse in her lap and peered over at me. "My aunt thinks you're trying to date me and wanted to quiz you about your intentions."

"Thank you for rushing me."

She laughed. "I told her it was just a business dinner, but she didn't believe me. Wanted to know why realtors needed business dinners and why you couldn't function professionally without someone to hold your hand."

"Wow. She must think highly of me," I said dryly. "Was that was the fighting was about?"

"Yep. She insisted on you coming in so she could check you out and ask you everything including the size of your penis. She said, and I quote, "Never marry a man with a small penis.""

I choked on thin air. "She said that?"

"That was when I ran. I don't want to hear anymore." She shuddered and adjusted so that she could look at me. "So, that's why I'm late. Also, know a good hotel so I don't have to go home tonight?"

I recovered, laughing. "It'll be fine. If you stay out, she'll just accuse you of sleeping with me."

"Yeah, you're right. And if I'm going to be accused of having sex, then I actually want to have it." She shrugged one shoulder.

I bit back another laugh at her. She seemed to be back to the normal Mallory I knew, and I was glad. The over-happy one had been weird.

I pulled into the restaurant's parking lot and put the car in park. I could have picked any restaurant in town, but I chose one that wasn't at the high end of the pricing.

I'd seen her this weekend. I'd paid attention to her as we'd walked around my parents' house, and she wasn't entirely comfortable with the ostentatious displays of wealth my mother was used to.

She'd be horrified if she knew that I'd brought a woman to anything less than the best restaurant in town.

Personally, I was happy with a date at McDonald's. Their burgers were the shit.

I got out of the car, and unlike when we were at her house, Mallory waited and let me open the door for her. It was such a small gesture, but it'd been ingrained in me from a young age to just be polite.

Hell, if someone opened the door for me, I'd be delighted. Nobody ever did that.

"Is this place good?" Mallory asked. "I've never heard of it."

"No. I'm deliberately bringing you somewhere where I know the food is bad."

"Shut up." She nudged me as I opened the door to the restaurant and motioned for her to go inside. "You don't have to do that, you know. The doors."

"I do." I gave her a small smile. "It's called being a gentleman."

"I know. I just wanted to let you know that you didn't have to."

"And I'm telling you that I do. Stop arguing." I touched

my hand to the back and took her to the hostess' station.

"Good evening, sir. Do you have a reservation?" The young woman asked me with a bright smile.

It was almost as bright as Mallory's had been this morning.

"Under Reid," I replied.

She scanned the book and nodded, picking up two menus. "Please follow me."

We followed her through the restaurant to a small table in the corner. A single candle burned in the middle of it, and I wished I'd thought to make a point that this wasn't a date.

Now, it was romantic.

Damn it.

I pulled out the chair for Mallory. She shot me a half-smile, lips just curled up, and took the seat. I knew what she was going to say, so I shook my head and cut her off. She could tell me that I didn't have to pull her chair out, but here we were.

I did have to.

And I wanted to.

I took my seat and the menu from the hostess. She smiled and said a waitress would be right over, then left us.

"So," Mallory said, opening the menu in front of her. "What's the real reason you asked me to have dinner?"

"You think there's a reason other than the fact I owe you dinner for helping me out?"

"Yes. Especially since you went all Cordelia Reid on me." She peered over the top of her menu at me. "Thank you for that."

I grinned back at her. "All right, there is a reason. I—"

We were interrupted at the moment by the waitress. I ordered a bottle of the house white, not that I'd drink a lot since I was driving, but one glass wouldn't kill me.

We ordered our food, and as soon as that was done, Mallory pinned me with a sharp gaze.

"Dinner. Why?"

I tapped my fingers against my chin and regarded her. Aside from the blue dress that hugged her stunning figure, her hair was still up in a bun—although a few more wisps of hair framed her face now—and her lips were just as red as they were this morning.

I shrugged one shoulder slowly, sitting back. "For what it's worth, I did mean that I owed you dinner. You did me a huge favor."

"It's my job."

"No. It's not your job to run around after me because I forgot to get the files and didn't plan my morning well enough. It's your job to answer phones and emails and schedule appointments and make coffee. You helped me a lot, and I appreciate it."

A light flush ran up her cheeks, and she glanced down. "It's okay. It wasn't a big deal."

"Your hair was wet."

"I'd just gotten out of the shower when you called. It was no big deal." She shrugged one shoulder and smiled at me. "It wasn't like you asked me to put on a theatre production. It was just some files."

"And an unfortunate incident in my kitchen."

That light flush became one that was a lot darker. "Cameron, I—"

"Look." I leaned forward, pausing right as the waitress arrived with our wine. I waved for her to pour it and as soon as she had, she left us, allowing me to dive right back into the conversation. "Look—it happened. You've been weird all day, and I knew you wouldn't be able to keep up that silly little happy act you put on."

"Weird?"

"Yeah. You were all happy this morning."

"Is it a crime to be happy on a morning?"

"No, but I've never seen you be it." I grinned. "Unless you've had two cups of coffee and half your body weight in carbs."

She gasped, pressing her hand to her chest. "What are you trying to say?"

"That you're human and you can't have had all that before you showed up today."

Groaning, she leaned forward a little. "All right, all right. I see what you're doing here. You want to talk about the fridge incident."

I barked a laugh. "Really? We need to refer to it as an incident?"

"Don't make this more embarrassing than it is."

"Why are you embarrassed? I'm the one who was practically naked."

"Because I—" She clamped her mouth shut after that. She shook her head, refusing to say a word as she picked up her wine glass and sipped.

"Mallory. Come on."

"I can't." She held up one hand and met my eyes. "It's just…awkward, okay? You're my boss. Maybe if I never had to see you again, I'd be able to tell you, but I can't."

I raised one eyebrow. "And you think you can work for me now knowing that I know you have a secret?"

"I don't—" She paused again, taking a deep breath. She eyed the wine glass as if it had something incredibly interesting inside it. Wine swirled as she tipped it side to side. "I don't think this dinner is a good idea."

I held up a hand just like she had to stop her. "The situation was embarrassing. Ignoring it isn't going to make it any better. I felt awkward, too. But if we're going to move forward, we have to address it, not ignore it."

She said nothing, and she still didn't look at me.

"Mallory, it's not like you walked in on me in the shower or jerking off or anything. I was in my towel, private areas covered, in my kitchen. It was partially my fault for not realizing that you're so damn good at your job that you'd take the bull by the horns and get me the information in a heartbeat."

Finally, she looked back up at me, indecision swirling in her eyes.

"You don't have to tell me why it's bothered you so much. Just drop the damn uber-happy act and know that one day, we will revisit this conversation."

"You aren't bothered that I practically saw you naked?"

"But was I naked?"

Her lips twitched. "No."

I held out my hands and grinned. "Then what's the problem?"

"I guess you're right." She visibly swallowed. "There isn't one. I just—I was worried it would be awkward."

"It's only as awkward as you make it. It happened; now we move on. Okay?"

"Okay." She nodded and pushed some hair behind her ear. "So this was to talk about it?"

I nodded. "I figured you wouldn't talk about it at work, so I decided to pull the dinner card and make you talk."

She rolled her eyes, once again picking up her wine glass. "Is that a Reid thing? Making people do what they don't want to?"

"Only if it doesn't hurt them." I winked.

Laughing quietly, she pressed one hand to her mouth and let her giggles fall into her fingers. "Great. Good to know my life isn't in danger, at least."

"Nah. Not yet, anyway."

She quirked a brow, but she smiled, her eyes shining a little. If she was going to say anything, it was cut off by our food being brought, and that was the end of that conversation.

SEVENTEEN

MALLORY

OUR CONVERSATION WAS WEIGHING HEAVILY ON ME.

Keeping my attraction to Cameron to myself felt wrong. Granted, admitting it probably wasn't a good idea either, but he knew I was holding something to myself. If I could get it out of my system now before it escalated into something more, then my job was not in jeopardy.

I could deal with it and move on. Part of that involved telling him. I wasn't entirely comfortable with that, but at least if I did it now, I could carefully choose my words.

I was going to do it. I was determined. I would tell him tonight, here at dinner, that I was attracted to him and had a girly little crush on him, but it wasn't going to get in the way of my job or affect how I was able to do it.

I was going to be an adult about this situation.

He had to know that my crush was why the fridge incident had bothered me.

I took a deep breath and finished my wine. We'd been long done with our food, and the clock was creeping close to eight-thirty. Between dessert and talking about anything and everything, from school to family to TV shows, the time had quickly passed.

It made it harder to actually tell him that I felt this way. I knew him on a personal level now. I knew that he'd graduated from college with a business degree and been an intern for his dad since he was fourteen, moving onto a paid position when he was eighteen, then to the place he was at now where he was in control of the business even though he didn't own it.

I knew he loved Game of Thrones, couldn't stand The Bachelor, and his favorite ever movie was Rocky Balboa.

We'd just…

Inner teenage girl sigh.

He was still my boss. I felt like he was my friend now, to an extent, and that was clearly the professional relationship he wanted us to have. That'd been clear from the start, actually. Sharing lunch, eating breakfast with me— he'd always tried to forge a friendship, and I was happy about that.

Cameron was such a bright, warm person that it was easy to be comfortable around him. More than anything, I wanted to work for him. And to do that, I had to be honest with him about how I was feeling.

That was the adult thing to do.

Clearly, my little miss sunshine act hadn't fooled him at all.

I sipped my wine and rested my hands on the table. "Can I tell you something?"

Cameron looked up from the bill, curiosity shining in his blue eyes. "Sure. What's up?"

"Uh…" I paused, fidgeting with the edge of the napkin in front of me. "What I said earlier wasn't entirely true."

"Are you telling me you don't actually like Harry Potter? Because that could be the nail in the coffin for this."

I laughed, somewhat nervously. "Oh no, you can pry my love of Harry from my cold, dead, hands. I just—earlier, when we talked about the fridge incident."

He slipped his credit card into the leather wallet that held the bill. "What about it?"

"I was so embarrassed because I have a crush on you."

I swear, he froze right at the same time I did. I hadn't meant to just…vomit it out like that.

I swallowed hard and met his eyes. "I am extremely attracted to you," I continued. "So seeing you in the kitchen like that was really embarrassing for me. It just reiterated the awkward way I feel about you, and I would really like if we could never speak of this. Ever. Never."

Slowly, Cameron pushed the leather wallet to the edge of the table, briefly dropping his eyes from me.

Regret pulsed through me.

Why had I said it? Why hadn't I let it go?

"Well, that explains the overly happy person this morning. By the way, that freaked me the fuck out." He looked at me. "Don't do that again."

My lips twitched.

The server came and took the leather wallet, much to my relief.

"Was that the thing you wouldn't tell me earlier?"

I nodded. "I didn't think it was appropriate."

"What changed your mind?" He looked at me thoughtfully. There was no judgment in his eyes, just genuine, gentle curiosity.

"Clean slate? I don't know." I twirled the wine glass between my fingers. "You said we'd have to revisit it, so I thought I'd get it over with now. Besides, I want to be honest with you." I let go of the glass and sat forward, then quickly sat back.

Sitting forward only reinforced my boobs, and that wasn't exactly helpful in this situation.

"It's not going to affect anything," I said quickly. "It's just what I said—attraction. It'll pass. It won't affect my ability to do my job."

"Hmm." He accepted the wallet back from the server

and thanked them. "Are you ready to go?"

I hadn't expected him to say he felt the same as I did, but the way he'd brushed it off still bugged me a little. I wasn't hurt, per se, but I was annoyed. He hadn't even acknowledged it.

"Yeah," I said. "Let's go."

I gathered my purse from by my feet and double checked that I had everything in there. I did, so I stood, pushing my own chair back in.

I was feeling too slighted by his outright dismissal of my feelings to care if he wanted to be a gentleman. And damn it, I'd open my own fucking car door, too.

I walked out of the restaurant ahead of him, not speaking. He was my boss, sure, but right now, that wasn't the positions we held.

Thanking the hostess before I left, I beelined for his car in the parking lot. I wasn't entirely sure which one it was, so I was more than a little thankful when he unlocked it and the flashing lights confirmed I was correct.

I got in the passenger side, with Cameron following me on the driver's side only seconds later. He hadn't even tried to get my door, so apparently he was smarter than I gave him credit for.

I didn't say a word as we drove. Neither did he. The silence was tight and uncomfortable, and I made sure I never made eye contact with him throughout the whole thing.

I was humiliated.

Completely and utterly humiliated.

It was just one more thing to add to my list to mistakes, and I was sure that tomorrow, I'd get to add my job to it, too.

What was wrong with me? Why couldn't I be a functioning fucking adult? Of all the men in the world, I had to feel this way about my boss.

My fucking boss.

Anger bubbled inside me. I could feel it, twisting and turning as it flooded my body with heat. The last thing I wanted was for my cheeks to flush in case Cameron thought it was about it, but it was inevitable.

I wasn't a pretty angry person.

The difference here was that I had to keep my temper if I wanted any chance of keeping my job. I knew he'd probably fire me tomorrow, but it was what it was.

I couldn't control it. I couldn't change it. I could only accept it.

Which was what I did as Cameron pulled up outside my house.

Without giving him a chance to speak, I unbuckled my belt and threw out a quick, "Thank you for dinner," as I shoved my way out of the car.

I wanted to wrestle my way inside. I wanted to lock the

door and run to my room, locking that door, too. Then I wanted to kick off my shoes, dump my purse, and throw myself onto my bed to cry.

Not because I was sad or heartbroken or anything. Crying was the ultimate stress relief, and I was faced with a situation I'd been in so many times before: being fired.

All I wanted was to move back out and get my life under control. I wanted to find love and keep it and not set anything on fire or cause any natural disasters in the process.

So I did just what I wanted to.

I went inside, bypassed my family entirely, and disappeared into my room, where I locked the door, took off my shoes, and screamed into my pillow until I cried.

And you know what?

I felt damn good doing it.

WITH MY HUMILIATION ALL CRIED OUT, THE NEXT MORNING, I DRESSED to conquer the world.

Well, not entirely. I was reasonably sure I'd need some form of weapon, and I probably wasn't the best person to entrust a deadly weapon to.

Instead, I wore my second-best dress which happened

to be a little black number that gave me the confidence of a thousand witches ready to rise against humanity. Paired with the heels I'd worn at the weekend and a red blazer, I slicked my signature red lipstick onto my lips.

Then, I looked into the mirror, nodded, and prepared to take on the world just as I'd intended.

The world wasn't really the subject, but a hot guy was most definitely just as tricky.

I arrived at work twenty minutes early so I could get myself sorted. A glance at the calendar on the computer told me I had two hours until Cameron arrived at the office, and I was going to use them to be the most efficient fucking assistant his ass had ever seen.

Starting with his desk.

I kicked off my shoes, grabbed a trash bag, and went into his office. The information was all so outdated, and his drawers were full of crap, so I busied myself sorting out everything in the room until I was satisfied it was up to the current year's standard.

I'd probably still missed something, but I'd been successful all the same.

I tied up the trash bag and left it in the corner of the kitchen before I headed back to my desk. I slipped my heels back on and got back to work.

I was already dreading when he got to the office. There was no way we could carry on like usual, and all I could hope for was that I didn't get fired.

I had big dreams.

Not.

I had a nervous tick. A bad one. Of tapping my right heel every few seconds, like my leg was hitched up to some kind of electrical resource.

Taptaptaptap.

It didn't stop until Cameron's familiar footsteps sounded on the stairs. Then, I froze, turning my body toward the computer and making sure not to look in his direction.

He didn't speak to me either, instead bypassing me entirely until he was in his office. The click of his door was loud and final and instilled an odd sense of hope into me.

Unless he was going to delay the inevitable, of course.

I didn't know. I was winging it. I had no idea how he'd take my cleaning of his office combined with the admission that I wanted to climb him like a tree.

Like I said.

Winging it.

I needed that on a t-shirt. If that wasn't an accurate description of my life, I wasn't sure what was.

Cameron's door opened again, and when I looked, he'd poked his head around it.

"Mallory? Can you come in here?"

No.

"Sure," was what I actually said as I stood and swiped my hands down my butt and over the backs of my thighs. My heels clicked against the floor as I carefully walked into his office.

He glanced at me as he pushed the door to, leaving it ajar, and sat down in his chair.

The chair I sat in was comfortable.

I was not.

I swallowed as he loosened his tie and undid the top button of his shirt, then sat back in his chair with a sigh.

"It's okay," I said quickly. "I know you're going to fire me."

Cameron's eyebrows shot upward. "Fire you?"

"Yeah. It's awkward, isn't it? We can't work like this." I shrugged one shoulder, even as sadness slithered through me. "It's fine. I understand. No hard feelings."

I got up and walked to the door. There was a squeak, and his hand grabbed my arm before I could leave.

"That sounded a lot more like a resignation than it did me firing you," he said in a low voice.

I shrugged again. "Whatever. I know what you're going to do."

"Do you?"

I tugged my arm out of his hand. "We've known each other ten days. My attraction to you makes my position untenable and this entire situation completely awkward. Of course you're going to fire me."

"I probably should." He spoke slowly, his gaze steady as it held mine. "It'd be easier if I did."

"See? There you go. It—"

"I wouldn't have to feel guilty about the fact I'm attracted to you. I wouldn't have to worry about what would happen if a relationship didn't work out. I wouldn't have to worry about anything other than dating you."

I tried to say something but…nothing.

Nothing came out.

Nada.

Not a damn thing.

My mouth was so dry that swallowing was a struggle, and I still couldn't talk.

Cameron sighed, lips curving up after. "Did you think it was one-sided, Mallory? The only reason I didn't say anything last night was that I wasn't sure if I should. I decided this morning that, like you, I had to be honest, so here I am." He held his hands out and shrugged. "I'm attracted to you. I think you're adorable and beautiful and funny, and if you'd like to resign so I can woo you without the complication of being your boss, I can't say I'd be sad to see you go."

I folded my arms across my chest at that. "Really? You'd have me quit just so you can date me easily?"

"No, I'd fire you, but I'm not doing that. I'm letting you

resign so you could date me."

"I'm not going to resign."

"I'm not going to fire you."

"Then what the hell do we do now?"

"You can do whatever you like, but I'm going to kiss you."

He took one step toward me and pulled me to him, then touched his lips to mine like a starving man. He swept one hand around the back of my head, and I melted against his body, curling my fingers into his jacket.

Heat—desire—tingled from the top of my head to the tips of my toes.

Something inside me told me this was wrong, that I had to stop it, but whatever that stupid little voice was had been overridden by the rest of my body. The rest of me was enjoying the fact that his lips were on mine and his hands were slowly pulling my body right against his.

And I was letting him.

His kiss was like magic running through my veins, and I wanted nothing more than to be under this spell until someone physically pulled me from it. All the frustration I'd felt last night, all the anger I'd harbored since I'd admitted how I felt washed away from me in one fell swoop.

I just wanted to live this—this kiss. Wanted to enjoy the moment of this, just in case I never felt it again.

Slowly, he pulled back, never releasing his grip on me.

"I half-expected you to slap me."

"I considered it after last night," I said in a low voice. "And I still might."

"I can take that." His lips brushed mine as he spoke. "Now what?"

"What do you mean, now what? You're the one who kissed me. You decide."

His fingers tightened their grip on me. "No. If I decide, we're both bunking off work today, because I'd like to toss you onto my bed and see if you slap me then."

I blushed. "Depends how hard you throw me."

Oy, look at me flirting! Ay-yai-yai!

He pressed his mouth against my forehead and silently laughed.

The decision was made for us when the phone rang from my desk. I was almost glad—I wasn't sure I was ready to decide what happened next, mostly because I had no fucking idea.

I'd expected to get fired. Instead, I'd gotten kissed.

I was taking that and running with it.

I was a little breathless when I sat down, and it wasn't because I'd run over here in heels. I had to take a deep breath and hope that steadied both my breathing and my rapid heartbeat as I answered the phone with my usual message.

I handled their request with ease, and when I put the

phone back down, I felt a pair of eyes on me.

Cameron.

He was standing in the doorway, adjusting his pants—something that made me fight a smile—and staring at me. "I need you to do something for me."

Uh-oh.

My mouth went dry. "What?"

"Those shoes. As hot as they are, I keep having visions of you breaking your damn ankle." He glanced at them and back up at me. "Change your fucking shoes."

He darted back into his office, leaving the door open.

And I laughed.

Then took off the shoes.

EIGHTEEN

MALLORY

"ARE YOU SERIOUSLY BRINGING ME COFFEE WITH BARE FEET?"

I wriggled my toes and put the cup down. "You told me to change my shoes, and I don't have any others with me. It's this, or I risk spilling coffee all over your desk again."

Cameron moved the mug and coaster a couple of inches away from me. "We both know you don't need to be wearing heels to do that."

"I know, but it reduces the risk even further. That's a plus."

"You know, there's a reason people say not to mix work and pleasure. Getting coffee from someone with bare feet might be it."

I laughed and moved so he couldn't see my toes. "I'm

not sure what that has to do with work, but if I'm ever in your kitchen, I can guarantee I'll be barefoot."

His lips quirked. "And pregnant?"

"Unless it's an immaculate conception, not likely." I raised an eyebrow. "Is this one kiss and you're laying out a future?"

"Not with you standing there with bare feet, I'm not." He snorted. "I hate feet."

"All right." I held up my hands with a shrug. "I'll go put the heels back on. I hope you're willing to carry me to the ER when I inevitably trip over a paperclip and break my leg."

"Just walk really, really slow." He paused. "How did you make it up the stairs?"

"Divine intervention."

"You took them off and put them back on, didn't you?"

I sighed. "Yeah."

His laugh was low and sent a little shiver down my spine. "Why are you even wearing heels? You wear flats every day."

"You notice that?"

"Of course I do. I look at your shoes so I don't get caught staring at your ass."

My eyebrows shot right up. "You've been staring at my ass?"

"I'm not even going to justify that with an answer." He

shook his head. "Just like you weren't talking to my belly button the other day."

I sat down in the chair reserved for clients and pointed at him. "Hey. It's not my fault. It's like a homing beacon down there."

He stared at me flatly. "Why the heels? Is it because you thought I'd fire you for wanting to get me into bed?"

"What is this? Is it open season for flirting here now?"

"Would you prefer I ask you to get out of my office?" He raised one eyebrow. "Or is it because you're not good at flirting?"

"How do you know I'm not good? I could be a master flirter for all you know."

He said nothing. Just blinked at me.

I sighed again. "Fine, I'm a terrible flirter. It comes with the disaster side of me. Honestly, I'm running out of good things to say about myself."

Cameron leaned back with a smirk. "You're a great sidekick when someone's being hit on."

"Ooh, yeah, that's what every man wants. For the girl he's dating to be good at stopping other women hitting on him." I paused. "Actually, that's not such a bad thing. But sidekick isn't a great term for it. And we're not actually dating, but whatever."

"We could be dating."

"We'd have to go on a date to be dating."

"So let's go on a date."

"It's not exactly the romantic dinner offer in the movies, is it?"

"Sorry. I'll buy rose petals next time."

I rolled my eyes. I was starting to wonder what I'd gotten myself into here.

Cameron leaned forward on the desk and gave me a lazy, sexy smile. "Come on. It's what we'd do if we didn't work together. One date isn't going to hurt."

I didn't think it was going to hurt if I told him I was attracted to him, but that had.

"I've only been here a week or so. Of course it's going to hurt." I hesitated. "It's not like I've been here six months and we're going on a date."

"So don't tell anyone." He lifted the mug to his lips. "We don't have to take out a billboard on the highway, Mallory. Didn't you listen to my mom's story about how she and her dad met?"

"Yeah, but I listened to like twenty of her stories that night, and they've all kind of blurred into one."

He laughed. "True. They dated for a year before they told anyone. Dad didn't know how my grandpa would react if he said he was dating his assistant, so they kept it a secret."

"But didn't they know each other before he hired her?"

Cameron shrugged. "Doesn't matter. They weren't close friends or anything—they knew each other in passing and because they moved in the same social circles."

"Which we don't."

"True, but you've met the women who move in mine."

"I have. Tall, slim, beautiful."

"And total bitches," he finished. "I prefer clumsy brunettes with crazy old relatives."

I pursed my lips. He was trying to systematically wear me down, and damn it, it was working. I'd been adamant from the start that this wouldn't happen because there was nothing more awkward than working with someone you'd broken up with.

"Okay, so we date. What happens if it doesn't work out? If you decide that the clumsy brunette with crazy old relatives isn't what you prefer?" I raised an eyebrow. "We still have to work together, right?"

He pushed up from his seat and walked around the desk, then perched on it right in front of me. "That might happen if you don't put your shoes back on."

I glared at him.

Laughing, he reached out and pushed hair behind my ear. "If it makes you comfortable, we won't go on a date. We'll just sit here in the office, behind our desks, constantly being attracted to each other while imagining the other naked."

"You imagine me naked?"

"Do *you* imagine *me* naked?"

"This feels like a trap," I said slowly. "I know—if we get to Friday and you still want to go out with me, I'll let you take me on one date, in secret, after work."

"You'll let me, will you?"

"Yes. I'll let you."

His lips curled into a smile that said he was more amused by me than anything. "You'll let me," he drawled.

That was all the warning I had before he leaned down, cupped the back of my neck, and kissed me so deeply I felt it all the way down to my toes.

I almost moaned when he pulled away because his kiss had felt so good. It was unfair. He was playing dirty and he knew it.

"You know the problem with growing up with money?" he asked with a tilt of his head and a curve of his lips.

"There are only so many ponies your parents can buy you before you run out of stables?"

His smile got a little wider. "No. It's that you're used to getting what you want. So I'll get you on a date. That, I can promise you."

"If you say so." I stood, then before I left, stopped right in front of him. There was a smudge of my lipstick on the corner of his mouth, and I didn't even think before I reached out and rubbed at it with my thumb.

The move was horribly intimate, and I drew in a deep

breath when I met his eyes. There was a fire in his gaze, one that made my stomach clench.

I stepped back before anything else happened. "Excuse me. I need to go fix my lipstick."

"Music to my ears." He grinned. "Also, you never did tell me why you were wearing heels today."

Damn it. I thought I'd gotten away with it.

I stopped in the doorway and turned. "Honestly, I really did think that you'd fire me, so I wore them to be this strong, independent woman, but then I realized I was afraid of tripping over my own feet, so that kind of negated the whole thing."

"You're really selling me on your good points, aren't you?"

"Eh, I make a mean sausage and bacon frittata. It balances out." I shrugged and smiled. "Cooking is about the one thing I can do without disaster."

"I like food. I'm sold." He grinned and winked, then stood up. "Now, go get back to work."

Rolling my eyes, I did just that.

THE REST OF THE WEEK FELT LIKE A BREEZE. WE'D SETTLED INTO A comfortable, slightly flirtatious relationship at work. It honestly helped that he wasn't always at the office, and I would be a liar if I said I hadn't been block-booking them so he'd disappear for a few hours.

Working with him was hard, despite how easy it was. He was right. If we hadn't been working together, we'd probably already be dating. I always knew not to mix work and pleasure, which was stupid considering I was the one who had.

I'd told him about my attraction to him and that had set this chain of events in motion. It was really all my fault, but it was going to happen sooner or later. And, if we were going to crash and burn because he realized I was way harder than he thought—and a potential walking fire hazard thanks to a flat iron—then I wanted it to happen sooner.

Because that would be what would inevitably happen. I'd seen the world he'd grown up in, and while I'd been far from broke growing up, it was a different thing. I bet he didn't eat breakfast around the table with his family in his pajamas, and I bet his aunt had never thrown a book at his grandfather because he'd called her a hussy.

Which might have happened last night.

Ahem.

I know. I thought they were only staying a few days, too. It'd been two weeks.

Whatever.

Now, it was Friday. Despite my reservations about

dating my boss, he and I and the world knew I'd go on a date with him. I was too curious not to, and beside the attraction, I was starting to like him.

Really like him.

He was funny. He made me laugh. He might have been in charge of the whole shebang here, but he never took himself too seriously. He didn't mind that I occasionally forgot to put his messages on his computer and sometimes left them in my desk, and he often watched with glee as I answered the phone to some of his…pickier…clients, and handled them like a pro.

I mean, come on. Great Aunt Grace was far worse than any of the people I'd spoken to on the phone since I'd started. Except perhaps his mom…

"I told you that you were going to bang him." Jade cradled her take-out cup of coffee as I set the machine to make mine. She didn't have any clients until ten, so she'd decided to stop by and get as much gossip out of me as possible.

More fool her. There wasn't any.

"I'm not going to bang him," I replied, watching the coffee splatter in my cup. "It's one date, Jade, and it's only because I'm dying of curiosity."

"Of how good he is with his penis?"

Yes. "No."

"You're such a liar. It's written all over you. Your born

again virgin-vagina is so ready for it."

"I didn't realize you had a direct line of communication with it," I drawled. "Look, it's one date. That's it. For all we know, we might not even be compatible. We may not get along as well as we thought."

"You've been talking about him all week. You get along fine."

All right, so that was a weak argument. "Flirting is one thing. It's another to date someone."

"Wait, you flirted and didn't scare him off? Wow. He must like you."

I turned and shot her a look. "Thanks for your support, douchebag."

"Oh, come on. You know it's going to go well. You're just worried because you've wandered in here, gotten the job, and now you've bagged the boss."

"I haven't bagged the boss."

"You're right. You'd need to get pregnant, and then you'd bag him for life."

"Jade."

"I know, I know. Shut up, Jade, blah blah blah." She rolled her eyes. "You're only feeling like this because dating your boss is so far outside your comfort zone."

"Well, yeah!" I paused. "Wait, what do you mean my comfort zone?"

She sipped her coffee and raised an eyebrow. "Mallory,

you have this little comfortable bubble you live your life in. You visit the same coffee shop every day. You always order the same bagel. You never go anywhere new, and you stick to everything you know."

"That's not weird. That's totally normal for most people," I argued. "Besides, any time I do something outside of my comfort zone, something goes wrong."

"It's all in your mindset, you know. If you assume that this date with Cameron is going to go badly, it probably will. You'll be subconsciously sabotaging it."

"And that's enough internet for you," I said, picking up my mug. "Now you're psychoanalyzing me? You're a hair stylist, not a doctor."

"You need one." She snorted. "Seriously. Don't go into it thinking that it's all going to mess up. It's going to be fine."

"I totally agree," said a decidedly male voice who wasn't part of this conversation.

Cameron stood in the doorway, a smile twisting his lips.

My cheeks flushed at the knowledge he knew I'd been talking about him.

"Oh, hey. What's up?" Jade said, unbothered by it.

"Morning," he replied, walking over to where I was at the coffee machine. "Are you distracting my employee?" He pulled a mug down, and I went to take it from him, but he shook his head. "Perfectly capable of making a coffee,

Mallory."

I rolled my eyes and stepped to the side.

"You bet I am," Jade said, replying to his question. "She wouldn't reply to my texts, so I came to talk about you in person instead."

"Ah, the best friend intervention." He glanced over his shoulder with a smile. "Are you going to subject me to questioning?"

Oh, my God. No.

"I like you. You're smart." Jade grinned. "Not right now, but I might have some after the date."

"Oh, so there is a date, is there?" Cameron's gaze slid to me, amusement shining brightly in his eyes. "Good to know."

"Don't you have to get to work?" I said to Jade, telling her with my eyes that she did.

Instead, being the insufferable little shit she is, she checked her watch and said, "Nope. I've got another ten minutes."

I ground my teeth together. "Of course you have."

Cameron's shoulders shook with quiet laughter, and when I glanced over at him, he was already looking at me with a smile.

I wanted to go to my desk, but if there was anything worse than being in the room while my best friend talked to my boss, it was not being in the room.

God only knew what she'd say if I weren't here.

So, instead, I sucked it up.

Not that anyone really said anything. It was mostly silent except for Cameron being polite and asking Jade about her job.

I stood and sipped my coffee, just waiting for her to leave. The following conversation with Cameron stood to be embarrassing enough as it was without her sitting here and deliberately causing tension.

And I knew that's what she was doing. She was a pain in the ass, and if I hadn't known her my entire life, I might just kill her.

After another minute of painful silence, she checked her watch and drained the last of her coffee. "All right then," she said as she stood. "I've gotta get to work. Mal, I'll call you later." She tossed me a wink, dumped her cup in the trash, and with a quick goodbye to Cameron, finally left us alone.

I blew out a long breath and shook my head.

"Wow. She's a character." He chuckled.

"She's a pain in the ass, and just so you know, she's part of the package. Trust me. I've tried getting rid of her. Still want that date?"

"A weird best friend doesn't change my mind." His eyes sparkled, and he put down his mug before standing in front of me. He gripped the edge of the counter I was leaning against and blocked me in so I had no escape.

"Are you sure? She's even weirder when she's drunk."

"So are most people."

He wasn't backing down.

"All right, that's it. She was my last line of defense." I shrugged and sighed. "I guess I'll let you take me on a date."

His grin was lopsided as he leaned in, quirking one eyebrow. The look was oddly sexy. "Tonight?"

"Tonight? Can't you give a girl some warning?"

"I did. I warned you on Monday I'd be taking you on a date. It's not my fault you didn't listen."

I opened my mouth to argue, but he was right, so I closed it again. He had said he'd get his own way, so…

"Whatever," I muttered, looking away.

He leaned in even closer to me. "What do you want to do? Dinner? A movie?"

"Aren't you supposed to decide? You're the one taking me." I looked up into his eyes and almost stopped breathing. His eyes were so bright, and there was nothing I could do but just stop and make sure my heart didn't beat right out of my chest.

Oh, I was in so much trouble with this man.

"All right, I'll decide," he said in a low voice, his thumb stroking my hip. "I'll surprise you."

"Okay, but can it include food?"

He stilled for a second. The laugh poured out of him,

and he dropped his forehead to my shoulder for a brief second. "Yes. There can be food. All good dates involve food."

"I completely agree. Can I wear yoga pants?"

"Why don't you just come to my house and I'll order pizza if that's the way this is going?"

"Your house seems a little personal."

"More personal than walking on me half-naked in front of my fridge?"

He had me there.

"Your house can be the second date." I nodded, reaffirming to myself that was the best idea. "Yes. If there is one."

"Nice save," he muttered, lips twitching to one side. "So I need to find a date that's outside, where there's food, and where you can wear yoga pants."

I tapped the side of my nose. "Good luck."

"Hurricane Mallory strikes again," he said under his breath, pushing off from the counter. "Blowing right through my plans."

I couldn't help but laugh at him. And I would never, ever admit that his stupid little nickname was growing on me.

Or maybe it's just because he was.

NINETEEN

MALLORY

"THIS IS A TERRIBLE IDEA," MOM SAID, CLOSING THE DISHWASHER. "Have you thought this through? Dating your boss?"

"We're not dat*ing*," I replied. "It's one date. What can it hurt?"

"Famous last words," Great Aunt Grace said. She waggled her finger at me. "There's something wrong with that boy, let me tell you, Mallory Harper. A young man like that, with money and looks, and he's still single? In my day that wouldn't be done."

"Yeah, 'cause you'd have snapped him up, you rotten golddigger!" Grandpa shouted from the living room.

"Watch your mouth, or I'll stick that cane where the sun doesn't shine!" she yelled back.

"Enough," Mom said wearily. "This is not about you

two and who used all the glue for your dentures."

Ew.

"Thank you, Mom."

"It's about Mallory and her terrible life choices."

Here we go. "It is not a terrible decision to go on one innocent date with Cameron. You told him you'd have him as your son-in-law, for Christ's sake!"

She turned fiery eyes on me. "If he weren't your boss. I specifically said those words."

"Fine. Then I'll quit, and then I'll be here even longer, long after Aunt Grace and Grandpa have gone, and you'll have to live with the knowledge that your grown-up daughter is living with you forever."

"If you quit, you can live with him," Mom sniffed. "And there's no need to be so dramatic."

"You're the one being dramatic," I pointed out. "It's one date. It's harmless."

The kissing wasn't harmless, but the date was.

That's right. I'd talked myself off the ledge of going out with him. Mostly.

"What if it doesn't work out?" She folded her arms across her chest. "Then what happens with your job?"

"It doesn't affect my job."

"You should get that in writing."

"It's one date, not a marriage proposal."

"It's a terrible idea!" Mom's voice rose a few decibels.

"He. Is. Your. Boss!"

"Say it a few more times, dear," Aunt Grace said, idly pulling the whiskey bottle from the bottle rack. "I don't think she understands that she's going on a date with her boss."

Mom shot her such a dark glare that it took everything I had to stop myself from laughing at her sarcasm.

"Look," I said, holding my hands out. "I went to his mom's mixer with him. We had dinner earlier this week—"

"Told you it was a date," Aunt Grace interrupted, slurping her whiskey.

"Wasn't a date." Now it was my turn to glare at her. "And nothing bad has happened. Absolutely nothing."

"Mallory, I don't want you to get hurt because you're making another bad decision. Think about Aaron—"

"We broke up two years ago, and it wasn't my fault he couldn't keep his penis out of other women!"

Aunt Grace cackled.

"Don't use that language in the house, Mallory."

"Sure," I said dryly. "I can't say penis, but you and Dad can have sex on the kitchen table."

Aunt Grace turned to her. "You had sex on this table?"

Mom waved her hand. "It's been disinfected," she said blithely. "Mallory, this is a terrible choice. If you want to be successful, you need to start making better ones."

"I don't know, Helen," Aunt Grace said. "Have you

seen that man's buns? Phwoar. That's a damn good choice right there." She even held up her hands and mimed grabbing someone's butt. "Also, she's wearing yoga pants. That relationship isn't making it past a hot dog."

I pinched the bridge of my nose. I should never have cracked. When they started asking me where I was going, I never should have caved, not even when Aunt Grace threatened to throw the lemon cheesecake she'd made in the trash.

Nope.

The doorbell rang, and I had to run to the door to get there before Mom. My yoga pants were magical things that had pockets, and my phone and debit card were already in them along with my house key. I was ready to make a break for it like I had before we'd had dinner the other night.

I wasn't so lucky. The second I opened the door to make my great escape with my hot boss, Mom was right behind me, gripping onto my sweater and stopping me from going any further.

"Cameron! How lovely to see you. Why don't you come on in before you kids head out?"

Kids? I was twenty-five! He was twenty-eight! What fresh hell was this?

Cameron looked at me, and I hoped that my wide-eyed, panicked look told him to *run away*. "Actually, Mrs. Harper, we really need to—"

"It's Helen, and nonsense! You can spare five minutes for a quick chat!"

"How tight are his pants?" Aunt Grace yelled.

"He could be wearing steel ones, and you'd still try to get in them!" Grandpa hollered back.

I smiled sweetly at Mom. "Do you still think he should come in for a chat?"

"I'm going to choke you on your dentures, Eddie!"

"Good, choke on yours and come to Hell with me!"

Oh, God.

"I think it's a great idea," Mom said, beaming. "Come on in."

"I think I'm going to kill you in your sleep," I muttered under my breath.

"What was that, Mallory?"

"Nothing. Not a thing. Just a prayer."

"You don't pray," Aunt Grace said, narrowing her eyes at me.

Clearly, she'd never seen me nursing a bottle of wine. Which, incidentally, sounded good right about now.

"Aunt Grace, this is Cameron. Cameron, this is my great aunt Grace." I waved my hand between the two of them.

Like the gentleman I knew he was, he took her hand and kissed it. "I remember. A pleasure to officially be introduced, Grace."

Aunt Grace fluttered a hand to her chest. "I think I need to sit down."

"Oh, Jesus," Mom snapped. "Cameron, how do you feel about tonight's date? Are you looking forward to being one of Mallory's terrible mistakes?"

"Mom!" I gaped at her. "You can't say that!"

"I can and I did."

Even Aunt Grace looked shocked.

Cameron, to his credit, didn't look flustered at all. "Well, I've already almost run her over, had her spill coffee all over my desk, and walk around the office barefoot, so we can just add it onto that list of mistakes."

"You told me to take off my shoes," I muttered.

"So you wouldn't break your neck, because I know you'd trip."

"I would not trip."

"You tripped over the stapler."

"I didn't put it on the floor, so I didn't know it was there." I folded my arms and huffed.

He fought a smile.

Mom watched the exchange with a frown. "Do you date all your employees, Cameron? Have you done it before?"

"Good God, no. That would have been incest. We used to share baths every now and then when we were kids, but we stopped that when she punched me in the eye."

"I'm sorry?"

"My cousin was my assistant before Mallory."

"Ah. So you waited for the first eligible young lady to come along and take her out."

"Not entirely. I was holding out for one who doesn't trip over her own toes, but they appear to be in short order around here."

Aunt Grace was watching the exchange with her whiskey glass in front of her mouth and a smile behind that. Cameron was matching her, barb for barb, and the best part was that she was insulting with him and he was rolling with it.

"I see. So you settled for Mallory," Mom said.

"I don't believe anyone can settle for Mallory. Or around her, actually. There's a reason I call her Hurricane Mallory."

Oh, God.

That earned him a cackle from Aunt Grace.

"Hurricane Mallory?" Even Mom looked like she was hiding a smile at that.

"Yep." He shrugged. "She blows through like a hurricane wherever she goes. She even gave me a list of demands for tonight which blew my plans apart."

"I didn't demand anything. I asked if it could be outside, with food, and if I could wear yoga pants."

"And I see you were serious about the yoga pants."

I looked down at the plain black leggings that hugged my legs. "I can change if you want me to."

"Nah, yoga pants work for where we're going."

"If it's a yoga studio, I'm leaving."

He laughed and shook his head. "Not a yoga studio." He looked at my mom and smiled. "We really do have to get going now. It was nice chatting with you."

With that he smiled, leaving my mom's mouth in a tiny 'o,' and guided me to turn around and leave.

Aunt Grace cackled as we headed for the door. "He owned your ass, Helen. I like him. We should keep him."

"I am so sorry," I whispered.

"Don't be. That was kind of fun." He winked at me, opened the front door, and we left.

"MINI GOLF. MINI GOLF FOR A FIRST DATE?" I ASKED, LOOKING AT THE wooden shack on the edge of the amusement park that was a few miles out of town.

"It ticks all your boxes. It's outside." He motioned to, well, the outside. "There's food nearby." He pointed at the amusement park where a cacophony of delicious scents were riding this way from. "And you can wear yoga pants." He pointed at my legs, then grinned. "I'm a genius."

"I wouldn't say you were a genius," I said slowly. "But it's pretty damn inspired."

"I'll take it. Do you want to eat first?"

My stomach rumbled. Loudly. "Eat. Definitely. There's some grease and bad carbs in there calling my name."

He laughed and wrapped one arm around my shoulders. "Let's go eat."

"Aren't we supposed to be keeping this secret?"

"Mallory, if you wanted to keep this secret, pizza and a movie at my place would have been the smart date."

Damn it. He was good at arguing. "Fine. By the way, I'm a little impressed with how you handled my mom back there."

He shrugged one shoulder and paid for us to enter the park. I'd never understood why the golf was separate from the actual theme park itself, but hey.

"We're already aware this is potentially a bad decision. She's just trying to protect you and, probably, piss me off a little. If I'd backed down or gotten angry, it'd reinforce her idea that she needs to protect you." He peered down at me. "You are prone to making mistakes."

"She basically called you a mistake."

"No, she called your decision to go on a date with me a mistake. Which, for all we know, could be."

"Are you changing your mind already?"

"No. But if I've learned anything about you over the

last two weeks, it's always to expect the unexpected." His smile reached his eyes. "I quite like your unpredictability. And, as I said, your clumsiness is kind of adorable."

"I hate it when you call me adorable." I glared at him.

"Tell that to your mouth."

I was about to tell him something, but I was so fixed on him I missed the rock. Stubbing my toe on it, I almost tripped, but Cameron was lightning-fast as he caught me.

Standing in front of me with a giant grin on his face, he brushed hair from my eyes and said, "See? Although I did expect you to trip at some point this evening."

I shoved him in the chest and shook my head, but I was smiling.

He laughed and pulled me right into his side, this time keeping a tighter grip on me as he grabbed my waist instead of my shoulders. I fit easily into his side, and it was so comfortable to wrap my arm around his waist, too.

It almost made me pause, how comfortable it was, but I didn't want to dwell on it.

We decided on hot dogs, fries, and nachos for food. He bought the dogs and fries; I bought the nachos and two Cokes. When we had it, we found an empty bench and sat down, listening to the rattling of the rollercoaster just behind the food stalls.

I watched as it reached the top then plummeted to the ground, a chorus of screams filling the air.

"You like roller coasters?" Cameron asked, picking up a handful of fries.

"I like watching people scream and plummet to their death," I replied.

He blinked at me. "That's a no, then."

I grinned. "Do you really think that putting me, the catastrophe queen, on a high-speed rollercoaster that could break down at any second is a good idea?"

A kid who was walking past us stopped dead next to our table and said, "Mommy? Is that true? The coasters can break down?"

The woman holding his hand glared at me and ushered him away, assuring him I was wrong and just a big scaredy-cat.

Well, she wasn't wrong about the scaredy-cat thing. The teacups were more my level. Those things could *spin*.

Cameron cough-laughed and covered his mouth as he reached for his drink. "No. I don't think putting you on anything mechanical is a good idea."

"That, and I don't like adrenaline. Well, I like adrenaline just fine, I just don't like doing the things that get it up. Like, why would you go on a rollercoaster just to be scared?" I shrugged and picked up a nacho loaded with guac and cheese. "If I want to be scared, I'll get up in the middle of the night and find my naked grandpa in the fridge."

"Did that happen?"

"I don't want to talk about it."

He laughed, picking up his hot dog. "You have a thing with finding men in fridges."

"I hope I never do it again. It's not a habit I'd like to make," I said with a firm look.

Cameron chuckled again, and that was the end of our conversation as we finished our food. Then, with full bellies, we threw away the trash and headed back in the direction of the mini golf.

I was bad at mini golf. And not little-kid learning how to play mini golf, I mean, *bad*. Given my natural talent for disaster, giving me a ball to hit with a stick was just asking for trouble.

Still, I was going to do well this time. Or I was going to try, and that was basically the same thing in my book.

As long as I didn't hurt anyone else, I'd be fine. And it'd be a better success than the last time I attempted to play...

I shook it off and took the ball and golf club Cameron handed me. Nerves fluttered in my stomach because he was probably about to see just how much of a klutz I was.

When he realized that, he'd nix this dating thing faster than you could snap your fingers.

I followed him over to the first lane and watched as he lined up his ball. It was relatively simple, as the first ones always were, and I hated it, but I wasn't surprised at all when he got a hole-in-one then stepped aside with a shit-eating grin for me to take my turn.

Like he knew.

He just knew I'd be terrible at this.

With a deep breath, I put down my ball and tapped it. Lightly. So lightly, in fact, that it barely even moved at all.

I didn't know it was possible, but Cameron's grin got even wider.

Yep. This was a terrible idea.

I tapped it again, and it went further, but still not close enough to the hole. All in all, it took me four more shots to get the ball in, and I was damn glad we were the only ones here.

"Well, this should be interesting," Cameron remarked, moving to the second hole.

"Shut up," I muttered, trailing along behind him.

And so it continued. He'd only need three shots maximum to pot his ball, but I needed at least three to get even close to the hole. Once, I even hit it so hard it went right out of the lane and I had to start again.

Honestly, at one point, I think he was contemplating getting up and going to get another hot dog while I potted the ball. In my defense, there was a damn hump and the ball did not want to go over it.

It was nothing to do with me. It was all the ball's fault.

"Wow. You really aren't good at mini golf, are you?"

He picked up his ball and smirked.

"Shut up. I'm not a sporty person."

"You're not a rides person, you're not a sporty person. What kind of person are you?"

"A lie in bed and watch Netflix until the judgey screen comes up person."

"I think we're all that kind of person." He laughed and positioned his ball to get his next shot. It'd probably only take him one freaking shot anyway,

I huffed and took a seat on one of the benches they provided which was, as I'd assumed, totally pointless. Two shots and his ball was firmly in the hole.

I stood and went to take my go. "Oh, crap. I don't have my ball."

"You didn't pick it up," Cameron said, grabbing his. "Although you should just give up now. There's no way you can beat me." He waved the scorecard in the air with a smug smile.

I glared at him as I turned toward the last hole. "Yeah, well—"

Those were my last words before my toes stubbed the lip that kept the balls inside the putting area. The rubber of my sneakers caught on the horrible astroturf-like stuff they used, and as I fell down, my ankle twisted.

I landed firmly on my ass. Pain shot through my ankle. "Shit!"

"Hell." Cameron dumped his things and dropped to my side. "Are you okay?"

I shook my head. "My shoe got stuck on the rubber. My ankle hurts."

He ran his hands down my leg in a move that was way sexier than it should have been given the amount of pain I was in. His touch was oh-so-light as he curled his fingers under the bottom of my yoga pants and gently touched my ankle.

Still, I winced.

"Come on. I'll take you to the emergency room to get checked out." He undid the laces on my shoe.

"Whoa, what are you doing?"

"If it's sprained or broken, it's going to swell. You need to take off your sock and your shoe." He gently pulled off my shoe, and then my sock.

"You're being awfully nice about my *bare foot*."

He chuckled. "What can I say? I have a hero complex that outweighs my dislike of bare feet. Hold these. I'll carry you to the car." He handed me the shoe where he'd stuffed my sock—white, this time—and picked me up like a Disney princess.

I giggled, then winced again. "What about the balls and clubs?"

"I'll explain at the booth. Let's go, Hurricane Mallory."

TWENTY

CAMERON

"YOU KNOW, IF YOU WANTED TO GET OUT OF THE DATE, YOU REALLY didn't have to sprain your ankle." I grinned at her in the front seat of my car.

She glared at me. "I was about to apologize for ruining our date, but now you can stuff it."

"I don't know. It was pretty exciting."

"Says the one who can walk."

Three hours at the ER had made for an extremely grumpy Mallory. As it was, it was now late, dark, and definitely getting cold enough for a coat.

I bent down and helped her out of the car. She'd already told me that under no circumstances was I to carry her again since apparently, that'd been a little dramatic.

Her telling me she thought she'd die from the pain was

dramatic.

She pushed the door shut and, with my help, hopped up the path to her front door. The house was completely dark, and when I took her key and unlocked the door, it was just as still as it was dark.

Nobody was here.

"Where is everyone?" I asked Mallory.

She slapped her hand to her forehead.

"Whoa there, Hurricane. I don't wanna be taking you back there with a concussion."

"Hilarious," she drawled, turning to look at me. "One of mom's favorite bands is playing at the bar tonight. I guess they took Grace and Grandpa, too."

"What bar?"

"Hook, Line, and Sinker."

"Never heard of it."

"It's not the kind of bar your social circle visits."

"Sounds like my kind of place." I grinned and gently squeezed her. "What time will they be back?"

"Uh… They'll be out until at least midnight."

"Really? Even your grandpa?"

She nodded. "Can I sit down? My ankle hurts."

I helped her inside and onto the sofa in the living room. "You can't stay here alone. You can't walk."

She waved her hand. "I'll be fine. I'll sleep here."

"You can't sleep on the damn sofa." I shook my

head. "You need someone to take care of you. I know what you're like. You'll get up and try to take yourself to the bathroom or something and fall again, and then you'll be screwed."

She sighed and dropped right back on the sofa, resting her head there. For a moment, she flung her arm over her eyes, then dropped it and looked at me with her big blue eyes. "What do you propose we do then? You stay here? Because my mom is going to explode if she gets home in the small hours of the morning and finds you here."

I shrugged and sat down in the armchair her grandpa usually sat in. The smell of cigar smoke was strong, but also, weirdly nice. "You could stay at my place."

"Let me guess: if we'd done pizza and a movie, this never would have happened in the first place."

I grinned instead of answering. She was in a bad enough mood thanks to the pain, so teasing her tonight was just going to get me on her bad side.

"If you come to my place, I promise to order pizza and let you choose the movie."

She sighed again, and I knew she was giving in. She didn't have much of a choice—she knew as well as I did that she couldn't stay here alone.

"Fine, but the pizza has to have pepperoni, and the movie has to be a serial killer documentary."

My lips twitched up at her demands. "If that means you won't get in any trouble, then fine."

"Wait. Where am I going to sleep? With you?"

I raised an eyebrow. "Do you want to sleep with me?"

Personally, I didn't think it would be a good idea. She was in no fit state to do in a bed what I wanted to do with her.

"I don't think it's a good idea. I mean, I want to, but it's not—oh, hell, this is going to shit."

I laughed at her and stood up. "I have a guest room. It even has a TV, and if you're nice to me, I'll let you eat pizza and watch serial killer documentaries in bed."

She groaned. "Now I'm a little turned on."

"Pizza and serial killers are the way to your heart?"

"Actually, nachos and serial killers are, but I'm not sure you can get nachos delivered."

I smiled and tapped the side of my nose. "Where there's a will, there's a way. Now, where's your room so I can get you clean clothes?"

Her eyes widened. "You can't go through my closet!"

"What? Are you going to stay in those until I bring you back tomorrow?"

"Yes?"

"What are you going to sleep in? Those clothes?"

"Yes?" Even she was wavering now. "Bring me back early. It won't matter. I'll sleep in my underwear."

I held up my hand to stop her *right there*. "Absolutely not."

She frowned, a cute little wrinkle forming between her eyes. "Why not? I sleep in my underwear a lot. Well, I don't wear a bra, but—"

"Stop." I pinched the bridge of my nose. Now all I could imagine was her sprawled across a bed, wearing nothing but a pair of panties. Of course, there was no bandage on her ankle, and the panties had flamingos on, but that was all I had to go on at this point.

It was more than fucking enough.

"Mallory, if you sleep in my house in nothing but a pair of panties, you're going to end up naked."

Her mouth formed a little 'o' of shock, and her neck flushed red as what I was saying sunk in.

"In fact, the only reason you're able to stay there at all and not end up naked is because of that." I pointed to her wrapped ankle. "So count yourself lucky. Want me to go get you some clothes now?"

"Actually, no, I don't, but I don't suppose I have a choice." Another sigh.

Good Lord, she was dramatic tonight.

"Besides, it's not like you've never seen my underwear."

I grinned and got up. "Exactly. Got any more animal panties up there?"

"Do not go snooping through my panties drawer!"

"I can't get any if I don't look!"

"Damn it!"

MY MOTHER STOOD IN THE DOORWAY TO MY OFFICE, GLARING AT ME

like I'd committed a cardinal sin.

I quietly sipped my coffee and motioned that she should come in if she'd like.

She did, gliding across the floor like she owned the room. Technically, she did. I just ran it.

She sat down with the elegance I'd known all my life, and I was ready. Despite her own fantastic love story she liked to share, I knew she'd wanted me to marry one of her friend's daughters, so I was prepared for the ball-busting speech I knew she'd come in to give me. I knew that she knew I'd taken Mallory out. One of her friends worked at the hospital, and she'd seen me carrying Mallory in.

I didn't care.

Sure, we'd discussed keeping our date a secret, but that had been blown the moment we'd gone out in public, never mind going to the hospital.

My mother was like the mafia. She had people everywhere, and they reported back to her like she was a queen.

And I just didn't care.

I couldn't care. I didn't have it in me to care. Mallory was growing on me in more ways than one—sure, she was clumsy and prone to accidents, but that was just who she was. She was also funny and kind and just the best kind of person to be around.

I wanted her. I wanted to get to know her more, to find out what she liked beyond nachos and serial killers and apparently, random trips to the emergency room.

Mom crossed her legs and linked her fingers, resting them on her knee. She was still staring at me, waiting for me to make the first move.

I wasn't going to. If she wanted to yell at me, she could make the first move.

I tore my gaze from her and back to the computer screen. With Mallory at home for the next three days, I had to take on a lot of her job. I'd directed the phone to Amanda's line downstairs, and Mallory had insisted on handling the computer work from her laptop.

I hadn't argued. She'd been pissed that she'd fallen asleep before she found out who the murderer was in her documentary, then she'd gotten mad that I hadn't paused it and just turned it off.

I practically choked her with painkillers until she cheered up.

I wasn't mad. Mini golf had been my idea, and I should have taken one look at that thing and known that the accident-prone woman I was starting to feel some very real things for would find a way to hurt herself.

For most people, that would be off-putting.

For me? Eh. Like I said: her clumsiness was adorable to me, mostly because she blushed every time she messed up, and I quickly realized that her blushing was like kryptonite to me.

"Oh, this is ridiculous. You're stubborn, just like your father," Mom finally snapped.

"Good morning, Mother. What brings you into the office on this fine Saturday?" I shot her a bright smile, employing Mallory's technique from earlier in the week.

Mom's lips thinned. "Don't play that game with me." Her expression softened. "How is Mallory?"

I raised an eyebrow. "How do you know there's anything wrong with her?"

"Olivia saw you carrying her into the emergency room last night, and I know you know that because you said hello to her."

"I did. I was wondering how *you* knew that."

"Don't be awkward, Cameron."

I sat back in my chair. "She's fine. She sprained her

ankle playing mini golf. Aside from being in a lot of pain, she's as sarcastic and dramatic as ever."

"I do like that about her," she mused, an almost dreamy look flashing in her eyes. "She reminds me a little of a younger me."

God help me, then.

"Great. We all need another you."

Mom rolled her eyes. "Cut your sass. I want to know how she is, that's all."

"And I told you. Sore, but otherwise fine. Now, why else are you here?"

She sighed and adjusted her sitting position so she was sitting up straighter. "You were on a date."

"Yep."

"I didn't expect you to admit it."

"Why? Because we work together? Because she's not one of your friends' daughters?"

Mom waved her hand. "Please. I gave up on that venture after Victoria and how terrible that date went."

Ah, the one where I'd called food poisoning from lunch and left.

"Well, four dates in two weeks was a little much, but I'm glad to hear it."

"Have you considered all the ramifications of dating her? I'm not being awkward, Cameron, before you say so." She held up one finger. "I was her once, but I'd known your father a lot longer than the two of you have known each other."

"We've had one date, Mother," I said. "We're hardly talking about having children."

"She stayed the night at your house."

"Because she sprained her ankle and when I took her home, there was nobody there because her family had a night out. I couldn't leave her alone, and it didn't feel appropriate for me to stay." I paused. "And not that I should have to justify this to you as someone who's thirty next year, but we slept in different rooms."

Mom sighed, slumping a little. "I like Mallory. I like her a lot, but don't you think she's a little...ditzy?"

"I don't think. I know she is." I grinned. "It's just part of who she is."

"Oh dear God, you're already falling for her."

I wiggled a pen at her. "I won't deny it. I want to see where things go, assistant or not. If you spent more time with her that wasn't on the phone demanding she come to some fancy-ass mixer, maybe you'd see what I see in her."

"Maybe I'll visit her at home. Bring her something to cheer her up."

"Oh, wait. She just emailed me."

"She's working from home?"

"She insisted on doing the emails." I scanned her email, then laughed.

She wanted to know who delivered her nachos last night so she could put them on speed dial.

"What's so funny?"

"I ordered her nachos last night, and she wants the number to put on speed dial." I typed back the number and told her I'd bring them with me tonight when I stopped by to check on her. Her aunt Grace had already said to me that under no uncertain terms I was to be the ultimate gentleman by getting her whatever she wanted since, in her worlds, the ankle was my fault for taking her to such a stupid place on a date.

At least her mom wasn't yelling at me anymore. In fact, she just about loved me for taking such good care of her "baby."

Man, it'd been fucking fun to see the look on Mallory's face when she'd called her that.

"Where did you get nachos delivered?" Mom asked. "That's a thing?"

"Yep. El Casa delivers them."

"Did she like them?"

"Like them? She hit me when I tried to take one."

Mom's face brightened. "Excellent. I'll go grab some now and take her some for lunch! That'll cheer her up, and I can get to know her a little more. Since you're dating."

"Mom, that isn't a—"

"Wonderful!" She clapped her hands and stood up.

"Mother, no, wait—"

"I do like nachos," she hummed to herself as she left.

My eyes went wide. "Mother!" I got up and chased her down to the front door, but no, she'd already gone. She moved so fast and disappeared so easily she was like a magical creature. "Damn it."

Amanda tilted her head to the side. "Was she muttering about nachos?"

I nodded, sighing.

"Huh. Can't imagine her eating nachos."

"She probably uses a fork," I muttered, rubbing my temples and heading back to my office.

This was a nightmare.

TWENTY-ONE

MALLORY

THERE WAS A KNOCK ON MY BEDROOM DOOR, AND MY MOM POKED HER head around it. "Doing okay, sweetie?"

I looked up from my perch on my bed. My ankle was raised courtesy of three poofy pillows my mom had sourced from her never-ending cupboard of things, and I had my laptop on a tray in front of me so I could work.

I couldn't lie here and do nothing while my ankle froze to death courtesy of two bags of peas.

"I'm fine. I'm hungry, though." I wiggled. "Ugh, this is so annoying."

Mom smiled. "You have a visitor."

My stupid little heart skipped a beat at the thought that it was Cameron.

And then it sank when I saw his mom.

It wasn't that I didn't appreciate her coming here, it was just that I knew it would be awkward. She was only here for one reason—she knew we'd been on a date.

I wasn't sure how she'd feel about it.

I wasn't sure how I felt about her being here while I was lying in bed, totally defenseless, with yesterday's mascara on.

Mind you, I suppose a bag of frozen peas would be a pretty nifty weapon in a pinch…

"Cordelia. Hi." I smiled. "What brings you here."

"Well," she said, stepping into the room with two boxes that smelled awfully familiar. "I stopped by to see Cameron, and he said you were feeling a little miserable, so I thought I'd get you some nachos and come and see how you were doing."

Wait—nachos?

Okay. I take it back. I was happy she was here.

"I'll leave you to it." Mom smiled and left, pulling the door slightly closed.

"Sit down." I waved to the desk chair. "Sorry, it's not great. I wasn't expecting company."

She slid her gaze toward me with a coy smile. "Except Cameron."

My cheeks flushed. "I was thinking of my best friend, but I guess he works."

Cordelia laughed as I shut my laptop and put it to the

side. She handed me one of the boxes. "I tried to get them to put some margaritas in take-out cups, but they were unfortunately reluctant."

"You can't get the staff these days," I replied, trying to hide my surprise at her desire to get margaritas in a take-out cup.

That was a genius idea.

"Hey, I see your face. I can let loose like every other person." She grimaced as she sat down. "I might not have done it for thirty years, but that was because, like you, I ended up with my ankle strapped when I'd done it—except it was a cast because I'd broken two bones."

My jaw dropped. "What? Don't tell me that you, Cordelia Reid, are a closet klutz."

"Is that so surprising?" She raised one perfectly plucked eyebrow.

"Yes!" I blurted out. "I mean, no. I mean, oh shit."

She laughed, putting her box on the desk. "I know. I'm put together. I'm uptight. I'm the epitome of the perfect hostess, no?"

"I wouldn't say—"

"I would. Say it. It's fine. It's an image I've cultivated." She opened her box and picked up a nacho coated in salsa. "Did you ever think you'd see me eating nachos?"

"I never thought I'd be eating anything but my words with you if I'm honest."

Another pearly laugh escaped her. "I like you, Mallory. I think you're a breath of fresh air."

Well, this was going better than I'd expected. Even after she'd pulled out the nachos.

"Oh. Well, thank you. Your son thinks I'm a hurricane, so at least you're complimenting me."

She covered her mouth as she'd just taken a bite of chip. "Yes, his father told me about that. Apparently, he'd been muttering about Hurricane Mallory, and it only figured that was you. I don't know any other Mallorys."

"Lucky for whoever wasn't named Mallory. It means unfortunate."

"Then you're aptly named, yes?"

My lips twitched at that. "I guess you could say it that way. So, Cordelia, tell me. How did you break your ankle?"

Laughing, she used a napkin to wipe sauce from her mouth and launched into the tale of trampolining gone wrong. Long story short, the safety net hadn't been there, and she'd accidentally bounced right off, first hitting her ankle on the hard metal of the frame and jarring it before landing squarely on her left foot.

I couldn't imagine Cordelia trampolining. Her hair was so perfectly in place, but the more stories she told me, the more I found myself liking her.

And I didn't quite know how I felt about that.

She stayed for around an hour and a half before she

left, saying she had a nail appointment.

When she'd gone, I sat in a daze.

Cameron's mom had just brought me nachos, told me she'd broken her ankle because she'd also been clumsy, then left without mentioning our date.

I didn't understand. I was totally confused about it, and the peas on my ankle were now completely defrosted.

I picked my phone from the nightstand and opened my text chain with Cameron.

Me: Is your mom sick?

I opened my laptop again while I waited for his reply. I'd been sure that Cordelia was about to tell me I couldn't date Cameron. Or that she'd do what my mom did; point out all the reasons why it was an absolutely terrible idea that should burn in hell.

She hadn't done either of those things. Why? She knew about the date. I was sure of it. Cameron had known someone at the hospital last night, which meant they probably knew his mom.

My phone buzzed as I opened my email.

Cameron: Why?

Me: She came over with nachos and told me stories

about her life before she had you.

Cameron: She did... what?

Me: Yeah. She tried getting the restaurant to give her margaritas in a take-out cup but they refused.

Cameron: I don't understand.

Me: I thought she was coming here to shout about our date.

Instead of replying by text, he called. I hit the green answer button, and he wasted no time at all diving into conversation.

"She came in here in a foul mood," Cameron said without saying hi. "And asked me about everything. She did it in a total roundabout, fucked up way, but she asked me if I'd thought through dating you."

"What did you say?"

"That we'd been on one date and we weren't planning babies."

I shuddered. "No, thank you. Well, she didn't say anything about it to me."

"That might be my fault," he said hesitantly. "I told her

that if she got to know you, she'd see you the way I see you."

"Which is…"

"What?"

"How do you see me?" A total hot mess. A walking disaster.

"You'll see."

I could hear his smile from here. "No fair."

"Life isn't fair. So she didn't go too hard on you?"

"No. She was almost like… my friend. It was weird. I'm not sure I liked it."

He laughed. "Yeah, she has this soft side she lets out sometimes. I guess she really wanted to get to know you and let her guards down."

"I guess she did. Does that mean she doesn't mind us dating?"

"I don't know. I also don't know if we can really call it a date if it ended up in the emergency room."

"A half-date?"

"Sounds about right. For what it's worth, I'm taking all sports-related ideas off the table. Unless you can hike?"

"Oh, hey! There's something I can do." I paused and glanced at my foot. "Not right now, obviously, but hiking is about the only sport I've ever been able to do without breaking a bone."

There was a slight pause from his end. "See, now you've

said that…" he trailed off.

"Shut up," I moaned. "This isn't fair. I can't go on dates to the movies for the rest of my life!"

"We can think of something."

"What about after you? When I marry you for your money and divorce you after we've had a baby to get child support?"

"Okay, first," he said, not bothering to hide his laughter, "You're so clumsy you're going to need a nanny, and my affair with her is probably going to be why we divorce anyway."

"Fair point."

"And second, you'll get custody because I'm a pig, so you won't have time to date anyone."

I raised my eyebrows. "Oh. So just because I get custody of our hypothetical children, I can't date? You'll have them at weekends, you know."

"That'll still give me three extra days to date."

"Ugh. I might have to rethink the children."

"Wise choice. They might get your inability to walk in heels and talent for knocking things over. I could never cope with two of you."

"I couldn't cope with two of me. Never mind you coping with two of me." I laughed, leaning right back against my headboard.

A wave of happiness flowed through me. At this

moment, he wasn't my boss. He was just a guy I liked, and we weren't thinking about a boss marrying his assistant, we were joking about a guy marrying a girl.

It made my heart happy.

Could hearts be happy?

That was such a weird phrase.

Hearts weren't a clitoris. Now, a *clitoris* could be happy.

"Can I come by tonight? I promise to bring dinner," Cameron said after a moment in a much softer voice.

"What dinner are you bringing?" I asked, curiosity getting the better of me. "And it's not like I'm going anywhere, is it? I'm hardly going line dancing."

"Can you line dance?"

"Not the point, Cameron."

"I like it when you say my name."

"Stop it, or I'll pull out the Mr. Reid card."

He barked a laugh. "Pull it and see what happens to you. Also, I'm bringing a salad."

What?

"A salad? Who the fuck brings an invalid a salad?"

"An invalid? Is that what you are now? Jesus, settle down, Mrs. Shakespeare. Save some drama for somebody else."

I covered my mouth with my hand to hide my laughter. "I'm a cripple! I can be dramatic."

"Stop it. I'll bring you food. Clearly, that's the way to

your heart."

"Uh-huh. Food and orgasms."

"Luckily for you, I'm good at giving both. See you later."

The bastard hung up, mostly because he knew he wouldn't be able to get the last word on that. That didn't mean I wasn't a: blushing, and b: going to pull out one of my rare good-flirt cards and text him.

> Me: If you give me good food, I might just let you give me what you call a good orgasm... And then I'll let you know.

"THAT IS THE WORST REASON TO MURDER SOMEONE. IT'S SO OBVIOUS."

Cameron put some popcorn into his mouth. "Life insurance? Really?"

"That was three million dollars!" I pointed at the screen. "I'd murder someone for three million dollars!"

He turned to me, one eyebrow raised. "Should I be worried?"

"Yes." I nodded. "I'm going to divorce you for screwing the nanny, take all your money, then murder you and get your life insurance policy. Bingo. I'm set for three lifetimes."

"From other people, that might scare me, but the only thing you can murder is carbohydrates."

"Maybe I'll kill you with them."

"Impossible." He trailed his finger up and down my arm. "You can't kill someone with carbs. It's like killing them with kindness. You might get a stomachache, but they won't actually die."

I sighed and leaned back into him. "Shame. I've tried to kill a few people with kindness."

"Really? You?"

"Do you want me to kick you out of my bed?"

"Technically, I'm on it, not in it."

"Only because Aunt Grace made you swear on the bible you wouldn't get in bed with me," I reminded him. "And I've seen you trying to creep under there."

He grabbed a handful of popcorn. "Yeah, but that's where your ass is. And where I can give you an orgasm."

I looked at my foot, then at him. "Seriously? I have frozen sweetcorn on my ankle. Is that hot to you?"

"I thought it was peas."

"I'm working my way through the frozen vegetable aisle. And what?"

"Nothing." His lips twitched, his shoulders shaking as he tried to hide a laugh. "No, frozen vegetables are not remotely attractive."

"Good, because I've had enough of this today. Can you take it off?"

He handed me the popcorn and removed his arm from around me to grab it. "What am I supposed to do with this?" He held the bag by the corner. "Re-freeze it?"

"Re-freeze it? No, you donut. You can't refreeze things. It's bad for you!"

"You're not eating this, Hurricane. You're using it so you can get back on your feet and stop annoying everyone." He grinned.

"You're starting to annoy me."

"Easy fix." He got up and tossed it in the trashcan to join the peas.

"What? Are you going to be quiet now so I can watch another episode of this show?" I grabbed the controller, but he was quicker than me, even making sure to mind my ankle.

He slipped back into place next to me, sliding one arm around me and tilting his body so that it mostly covered mine. His large hand framed my face, but it was his lips touching mine that proved his point.

My fingers loosened until the controller dropped, and I sank my fingers into his hair, letting him prove whatever point he was trying to make. It felt like it'd been forever since he'd kissed me in his office, and I guess it had. Almost an entire week.

Why did that feel like an eternity?

This was spontaneous, intense—utterly thrilling. Shivers covered my entire body, and each stroke of his tongue against mine set me on fire.

For a second, I almost forgot how much my ankle hurt, how frustrated I was to be lying here resting, how badly I wanted to eat the rest of the pizza in the box on the desk.

There was just Cameron. Just his fingers winding in my hair, his lips moving over mine, his body hot and hard beneath the t-shirt that covered his abs.

Just the steady, thumping beat of my heart as he took expert control of my body without barely touching me at all.

I fell into it. Let it happen. It was just a kiss, but it was a kiss that meant so much. It was the kiss that crossed the line, well and truly, between co-workers and lovers.

It was the one that made me realize… Maybe I didn't care.

Maybe I didn't actually give a crap that he was my boss. I knew that anyway, but now, as he kissed me, I realized that the maybe wasn't such a maybe.

His kiss gave me life, and it felt so damn good that I didn't care about anything. I just wanted to keep kissing him until I either couldn't anymore or I passed out.

Slowly, much to my chagrin, he pulled away, keeping his hand curled around the back of my neck. "Still annoyed?"

I shook my head, releasing my hold of his hair. My fingers trailed down the side of his neck, and I curved them so they ran along the stubble that coated his jaw. It was coarse and rough, tickling across my fingertips.

His lips pulled to one side as I did it, and I found that mine did the same.

"I have an idea," he said in a quiet voice. "How about we have another date when you're able to walk? A proper one, with food, indoors, and serial killers?"

"Sounds like we're having one right now," I whispered back, leaning forward to kiss him again.

TWENTY-TWO

MALLORY

"GOOD AFTERNOON, YOU'VE REACHED CAMERON'S REID'S OFFICE AT REID Real Estate. Mallory speaking, how can I help you?" I held the phone to my ear and typed at the computer.

It was two days since Cameron had kissed the hell out of me in my room. Two days in which he'd visited me after work, brought me food, watched serial killer documentaries with me, and kissed me breathless before he'd left.

Now, I was able to put a little weight back on my ankle, and I'd insisted on coming into the office because I was getting a severe case of cabin fever. Not to mention there was only so many more times I could hear Aunt Grace tell me about her days as an acrobat while complaining about mom's "stupid little poofy dog."

So, Cameron and I had compromised. Meaning I now

had a footstool beneath my desk which, actually, wasn't so bad.

Quite comfortable.

"All right, thank you very much, and we'll see you next week, sir." I hung up right as fingers brushed across the back of my neck. A shiver shot down my spine as Cameron kissed the side of my neck. "What are you doing?"

"Kissing your neck," he murmured, doing it again. "Is there a problem?"

"Yes, I'm working." I squirmed beneath his touch, even though I liked it. "I have to put this appointment on the calendar before I forget, and you miss it."

He sighed and stood up. "Well, that ruins my hot way of asking you for a date tonight, doesn't it?"

"Really? Sneaking up behind me when I'm on the phone is your way of asking me out?"

"I think we've made it past the part where I ask you and more where I tell you."

"Tell me, huh?" I saved the entry into the calendar and spun in my chair so I could face him. "You don't tell me a thing, mister."

I got up and walked to the kitchen.

Walked was a vague term.

I hobbled.

"If you're trying to get away from me, you really need to rest that foot for at least another day," Cameron said, following me in there. "Otherwise, you're hobbling around like a one-legged leprechaun looking for gold."

"I have two legs, thank you."

"I have noticed."

"Are you here to work, or just flirt with me?"

"Hey, it's the first time in three days you've been in the office. Do you know how quiet it is without you when you're not here?"

"No," I said slowly, hitting the button for the coffee machine. "But I imagine there isn't coffee spilled everywhere."

Cameron hesitated. "I may have knocked over my cup yesterday."

I gasped, turning around to face him. "You!"

He grinned, quickly closing the distance between us and pinning me to the counter. "I didn't. I just knew you'd turn around."

I glared. "Don't annoy me."

"Oh, come on." He leaned right in and brushed his lips over the corner of my mouth, eliciting a shiver from me despite my protestations.

"You aren't playing fair. You know what happens when you do that." I pushed at this chest.

"Mmhmm. You don't get annoyed with me." He dragged his lips over my jaw and down to my neck. "You forget I was ever getting on your nerves."

Yes, but—

"Not fair," I whined, sliding my hands down his chest. "Why were you getting on my nerves?"

"Ha, bingo!" He stepped back and gripped the counter, still keeping me in place. "See, you've forgotten everything."

I narrowed my eyes and looked at him. "No, I haven't. You were kissing me when I was trying to work. Then you kept on distracting me, and all I wanted to do was work…"

"Yeah? If I come to you right now, are you gonna push me away?"

"I didn't say that." I couldn't help how my lips curve. "But wasn't there something about a date when I could walk again?"

Cameron paused at that. "I said that at your house, right? Before I kissed you and wanted to do a hell of a lot more."

"You could have ended that with "at your house, right?"" I raised my eyebrows and pulled the first mug from beneath the coffee machine and made it the way he liked it, then handed it to him.

He smiled as he took it. "I could have, but I decided not to."

"Clearly." I put my mug under the machine and hit the button before I turned again. "But, yes, then. You owe me a date and, like, a pound of chocolate for the pain you've put me through."

"Yeah, it's all my fault. I know." He laughed and nodded toward the machine. "Your coffee is done."

"Can you finish it for me? My foot hurts." I pulled out a chair at the little table in the center of it to make my point.

"Are you all right?" He glanced at my foot before putting down his mug and moving to finish mine.

"Sore. It's the first day I've really been using it a lot."

He stopped in front of the coffee machine, and I made my move.

I trapped him against the counter the way he'd caught me, except I was pressed against his back, not his front.

Shit. There was a flaw in my plan.

"What are you doing?" Amusement was rife in his tone.

"Trapping you," I replied, deflated.

"It didn't work, Hurricane."

"I know that." With a sigh, I stepped back and dropped my hands. Damn it. I wasn't exactly the best seduction move I'd ever pulled. Then again, I wasn't good at any kind of seduction, so what was I doing?

Making a fool of myself.

That's what I was doing.

Story of my life.

Cameron turned around and looked at me, leaning against the cabinet. His half-smile was super sexy, and I knew exactly what he was doing.

He was letting me trap him.

Putting on my best strut—which was about as sexy as a baby llama—I walked toward him and, well, let's be honest. I didn't trap him. I more flung myself onto him and lifted my sore ankle off the ground while I slumped against him.

"Ah. So sexy," he remarked, lips against the top of my head.

"My foot hurts," I muttered into his arm.

"Then sit down, woman." He hugged me for a second before depositing me on a chair. "Rest your damn ankle. Stop being superwoman."

"I can't help it. I don't like to be babied."

"You were fine when I was bringing you food."

"Well, yeah." I met his eyes as he handed me my coffee. "You were feeding me, and you let me touch your abs. That's a kind of babying I can get on board with."

He half-smiled. "How about I bring you coffee and you touch my abs?"

"It's not food, but it's not bad. I can't sit here, though, in case my phone rings."

"I can answer the phone."

"Even if it's Cynthia Carlton?"

He hesitated. "Let's get you back to your desk." He hauled me out of the chair and helped me back to the desk.

I rolled my eyes. I could walk, it just hurt a little. Then again, I already knew about his hero complex, so I let him have his moment. As long as he never, ever picked me up again.

There was something disconcerting about it.

I slid into my chair right as the phone rang again. I answered, then winced at the voice on the end. It was Cynthia Carlton, and even Cameron could hear her through the speaker.

Slowly, he backed toward the kitchen, ready to get our coffees instead.

"No, he's available," I said brightly, grinning at him. "Let me put you on hold, and I'll patch you through."

"Thank you, darling!"

I put her on hold and grinned, stretching my arm out. "It's for youuuuu."

"Note to self," he muttered as he approached me. "Don't play dirty at work."

"I HAVE TO SAY THAT I'M PROUD OF YOU," CAMERON SAID, HANDING me a glass of wine.

"You are?" I looked up from my spot on the sofa. "Why?"

He sat down and gently rested my sore foot on his lap. "You couldn't walk and you didn't mess anything up."

"Yeah, I think it's because I have to be careful. Also, finding out your mother is a closet klutz might have inspired something inside me."

"Number one on things not to say to a guy you're dating." He slid his gaze to me. "I assume we've moved past the "It's just one date," line by now?"

"Have we had more than one date?"

"We've had two."

I leaned over and put my wine on the coffee table. "Technically, we've had several."

He frowned, resting one arm over the back of the sofa. "How have we had several?"

I started counting them off on my fingers. "You could count the mixer as one. Dinner as another. Technically the golf counts, even if it did have a tragic end."

"The Oscars are ready for your nomination, madam."

I poked my tongue out at him. "And all the times you've been at my house this week, plus tonight."

"Wait. You're counting the last few days as dates?"

"Why wouldn't I? You brought food, we spent time together, and there was a lot of kissing. Sounds like a good date to me."

He scratched his jaw. "I'm starting to think that you'll date anyone who brings you food."

"In a New York minute."

Laughing, he reached over and toyed with a lock of my

hair. "All right, so that's what? Six dates?"

"Seven."

He shifted, being careful not to hurt me. "Do we really have to count lying in your bed watching serial killer docs as a date? It doesn't sound like a date."

Whoa. They were fighting words.

"Okay, whoa." I held up my hands. "If you don't think nachos and serial killer documentaries make for a perfect date, I don't think I can be in a relationship with you."

He snatched my hands, linking our fingers together, then moved up the sofa so I was practically sitting on his lap. His lips were twitching as he tried to hide a laugh, and I stared at him with my eyebrows raised.

"I never said it wasn't a perfect date, even though you do argue with me when I'm right about the murders being stupid."

"That's your opinion, and in my opinion, it's wrong."

He licked his lips, not bothering to hide his smile this time. "I didn't plan for any of that to be a date. Honestly, I just liked lying there with you, watching TV, doing absolutely nothing. No expectations, no deep talks about the future."

"We did discuss me murdering you for your fortune and your life insurance."

Cameron paused, then wrapped his arms around me and held me against his body. "How long do I get you before you kill me?"

"Depends when we have children. Ideally, I'd like them to be adults so I can find myself a toyboy and run off to a private island."

He buried his face in my hair, his whole body shaking with his laughter.

"You won't be laughing when you're dead," I whispered dramatically.

It only made him laugh harder. He had the most infectious laugh. It was naturally deep but happy, and he was the kind of person who could start a Mexican wave of laughter.

"Is it wrong that I prefer this over the dinner we just had?" he asked quietly, pushing hair from my face so he could see me. "Maybe we have had seven dates."

I shrugged one shoulder and picked a little fluff off his white t-shirt. "The best dates are the ones that don't feel like dates at all. Sure, you can get dressed up and go to a fancy restaurant, or the movies, or whatever else people do when they date, but how much do you learn about a person? You can't talk if you're in the movie theater. You spend half a dinner date with food in your mouth. Bars are loud and busy. I've learned far more about you in the last few days just by lying and doing nothing with you than I would have if we went out."

"It's also a lot safer."

"That is an added bonus, yes." I smiled.

He brushed his thumb down my cheek. "You don't know anything about me, though. Not how you would on a date."

"I know that I like spending time with you. I know that I'm comfortable with you and I'm happy when I'm with you. Because of those things, I also know that I don't care anymore that you're my boss. And I think they're more important than knowing what your favorite food is or what you do in your spare time. I can learn that. I can't learn to want to be with you."

Gently, he cupped my chin, drawing my face close to his. His lips brushed over mine a few times, the lightest of kisses. "From a girl who plans to murder me in twenty-five-years, that was deep."

"Way to ruin the moment."

Giving a gentle chuckle, he kissed me again, this time more firmly. "I think it all makes total sense. I know that I want to be with you, too. Even if it means some expensive ER bills."

"Gee, thanks. Spend all the money I intend to inherit from your death on medical bills."

"Then I'll buy a big roll of bubble wrap and wrap you in that instead." He grinned, rubbing his thumb over my bottom lip. "So what are you saying? Are we going to give this a shot?"

"One condition."

"Which is?"

"If we break up, I keep my job, and you leave instead."
I winked.

Laughing, he leaned in again. His breath tickled my lips,
and my heart skipped a beat as I waited for him to kiss me.

It was hard to believe that, three weeks ago, I didn't
even know this man. That our first interaction had been him
helping me up from the side of the road after I'd
interviewed to be his assistant, unbeknownst to us both.

It was crazy to think that he wanted me despite all my
little quirks. That he embraced my natural clumsiness so
much to call me 'Hurricane.' That it was cute and amusing
to him.

It was even crazier to think that he was my boss.
Nobody in the office even knew, thanks to us having the
top floor. It was easy to forget that we weren't the only two
people in the building, but maybe that would make it easier.

I just had to hope that it didn't all go to shit one day.

But the thing was, for someone who really didn't
venture outside of her comfort zone for fear of screwing
things up, this felt big. Because he made me feel brave, and
there was a part of me that believed this could work.

That belief only strengthened as he finally kissed me. It
was deep and slow, the kind of kiss that curls your toes and
sends goosebumps dancing over your arms. I reveled in it,

kissing him back as my heart pounded against my ribs and an ache grew between my legs.

I clenched my thighs, and as if he felt it, he pulled back.

Cameron searched my eyes. "We're past the three-date rule, aren't we?"

I nodded. "And I didn't wear matching underwear for nothing."

"How are you with stairs?"

TWENTY-THREE

MALLORY

TURNED OUT, I WAS NOT GREAT AT STAIRS TONIGHT.

Halfway up, Cameron practically picked me up over his shoulder because I was taking too long. I didn't even complain.

Like I said. I'd put on matching underwear for a reason. Women didn't do that unless they wanted someone to see it.

I lay back on the bed. Cameron climbed over me, instantly kissing me. Heat flushed through my body as his covered mine, and I wound my fingers in the soft fabric of his shirt.

It tugged up, and I kept pulling it until it was right under his arms. He paused kissing me long enough to yank it over his head and toss it to the side.

My fingers explored his body as he kissed me, running up and down the muscles that made up his stomach and his chest. They were everywhere, and I shivered a little in delight as he deepened the kiss.

Heat pulsed through my body. I wanted him so bad. I hadn't realized just how badly until now.

As if he could read my mind, he moved. He was so careful not to knock my foot as his mouth trailed from mine, peppering kisses over my jaw and down onto my neck. Controlling my breathing was becoming harder and harder, and his lips brushed the tender, sensitive spot below my ear.

I gasped as he moved further, curving his hands into the straps of my dress and pulling it down my body. Thank God it was stretchy and easy for him to remove.

He pulled it off and threw it to the side. His eyes raked over my body, lingering on the black lace underwear set I'd put on. Moving back to me, he ran his hands up my legs, leaving goosebumps in his wake, and kissed me once more.

I arched my back into him as I returned the kiss. His skin was hot to the touch, and I had no doubt that mine felt the same.

He returned to his exploration of my body with both his hands and his mouth. His lips were soft, his touch firm. His fingers probed every inch of my upper body, culminating with him snapping the front clasp on my bra and pushing the cups aside.

He took his time exploring those, too, with his tongue and his fingers. His tongue swirled around my nipples, one after the other, sending desire shooting right through me.

I didn't want him to stop, but at the same time, I wanted more. I wanted to feel more because the throbbing of my clit was getting close to unbearable.

It was like he knew that, too, because he moved to the side and slid one hand between my legs. I was completely wet, so much so that he could probably move inside me right now without touching me again, but the way he moved his fingers told me that wasn't going to happen.

I gasped and bucked my hips as his finger found my clit. He smiled against my skin, kissing back up my neck as he circled it. Once again his lips covered mine, but his hand didn't move, except to tease and rub my clit.

I was going to come, and he knew it.

I grabbed the sheets with one hand and held his mouth to mine with the other. The pleasure quickly built inside me and slammed into me just as fast. It was a quick and furious orgasm that wracked my entire body with a series of shudders.

Cameron's chuckle into my mouth made me blush before I realized how ridiculous that was. "That was easy."

"Clearly you have better things to do with your mouth than talk," I snapped back, slightly breathless.

"I do, but I'm not giving away all my secrets right now." He dropped another kiss to my lips, dragging his teeth over my lower lip as he released me.

He reached into the nightstand, and I propped myself up on my elbows to see what he was doing.

All right, I was looking at his abs.

Still, that didn't stop my gaze from wandering as he pulled down his pants and his boxer briefs.

And then I coughed and blushed, looking away.

His laugh was deep, and it tingled over my skin, making me shiver. I heard the rip of a condom packet, and a few seconds later, he was leaning over me again.

This time, his hand was on my good leg, lifting it to hook over his hip. His other was on the side of my head, and his lips claimed mine as he released my leg to reach between us.

The head of his hard cock moved through my wetness, making me twitch when he brushed over my sensitive clit, and slowly, pushed his way inside me.

My chest arched again, and that made his lips brush over my neck once more as my head went back. He moved so slowly, almost testing it out, easing his way into me. Each movement sent a thrill through me, making my heart beat until I didn't think it could go any faster.

I kept one and around his neck and kissed him, then used my other hand to grab my bad leg and hold it up. He hummed his approval into my mouth and moved faster until all I could hear was the mingling of our labored breathing and the slapping of skin on skin.

I clenched, and he groaned, moving into me harder. I tilted my hips and got lost.

Lost in the movement of our bodies, in the sweat that coated my skin in a sheer sheen, in the way it felt when he kissed me as I came. He grunted as he joined me a few seconds later, and when he dropped his forehead to the bed next to my head, I let my legs fall.

He snuck one arm under my body and held me, and I wrapped mine around his neck. And we stayed like this for a few minutes, just being, just breathing, and I knew without a shadow of a doubt that I was falling for him.

"ARE YOU EVER NOT HUNGRY?"

I put another fry in my mouth and grinned.

Cameron shook his head and adjusted his boxer shorts. "How is it that you're lying there with your hair looking like a bird has nested in it, no make-up, and my t-shirt while you're eating your second dinner, and I still want to flip you over and fuck you again?"

I swallowed and reached for my wine from the nightstand. "If you do that, can you make sure you move the food first?"

He shook his head, but I knew he was laughing. "Where do you put it?"

"The extra ten pounds on my hips," I replied, grabbing more fries. "I eat salads for lunch. I keep a balanced diet, for the most part."

"I've only ever seen you eat junk food. I've never seen you eat a salad."

I shrugged. "I go out for lunch most days. There's this great little sandwich shop just tucked away from Main Street. It's run by this great Italian family, and as well as having the best meatball subs ever, they do awesome salads."

"Are you sure you're just having the salad?"

"Are you just jealous I've never brought you one of those subs?"

Cameron paused. "Yeah, kinda. Can we go there for lunch tomorrow?"

"I go there every day. I basically have a loyalty card. Two weeks in a row and my salad is free." It was my turn to pause. "Do I have to get you lunch every day now?"

He laughed. "No. Why? Are you concerned we'll spend a little too much time together?"

"It does seem like a lot."

"We'll be fine." He reached over and smoothed down my crazy hair. "I'm not always in the office, am I? Like tomorrow. I have an attorney meeting in the morning and a viewing forty-five minutes away in the afternoon. We won't see each other for most of the day."

"What about after work?"

"Are you busy?"

"No. I'll meet Jade for lunch."

He shrugged and leaned over to kiss me. "There you go, then. Problem solved. Don't overthink it, Hurricane. If you ever get sick of me, just tell me to leave you alone."

I stared at him as I grabbed more fries. "Like I'm going to get sick of you. It's far more likely that you'll get fed up with me and my clumsiness than it is the other way around."

"I can absolutely tell you that I will never find your clumsiness anything other than adorable." He tapped my nose. "It's a part of you, and you'd be far more boring without it."

"Are you calling me boring?"

"That came out wrong." He grimaced. "Wanna watch some serial killers?"

I narrowed my eyes. "You're trying to distract me."

"Is it working?"

Yes. "No."

"Liar."

"Shut up and put on some murder. I need some more ideas to plot yours." I picked up a small square of the pizza in between us. "See if I can combine some to get some ideas."

He chuckled and turned on Netflix. "Maybe I'm secretly plotting yours to stop you getting your hands on my money."

"Nah, it's easier if we just never get married and have kids for you." I shrugged one shoulder. "Why go through the hassle of getting married just to murder me?"

"You're planning the same."

"Ah, yes, but all I have in the bank is two-hundred-and-twenty-three dollars. I bet you're not interested in that."

"People have killed for less. Like the guy on the episode we watched last night. That was over a hundred bucks."

"A hundred bucks and a kilo of cocaine," I added. "I do not have a kilo of cocaine stashed anywhere. If I did, I'd be a hell of a lot richer."

"Or you'd mistake it for sugar and start getting me high at work." He glanced at me with a small smile.

I wanted to deny it, but... "Yeah, probably. Ooh, put that one on." I pointed to the tv with a fry. "I haven't seen that yet."

"Is this my life now? Take-out in bed with you in my t-shirt controlling the TV?" His tone was exhausted, but there was a twinkle in his eye that said he didn't mind in the slightest if it was.

I didn't mind, either. He'd been right—he was good at giving and orgasms. Very good.

I grinned and held up my pizza. "You bet your tight ass it is."

EPILOGUE

CAMERON

EIGHTEEN MONTHS LATER

"GOOD MORNING, CYNTHIA!" MALLORY SAID BRIGHTLY, SITTING FROM behind her desk. "How are you?"

Cynthia Carlton removed her winter hat and gloves and shook snow from her shoulders. "Hello, darling. I'm absolutely freezing. It's horrible out there."

Mallory nodded. "It is. Here, come sit down, and I'll get you a cup of coffee."

"I got it." I walked out from where I'd been lurking in the hall and put Mal's coffee on her desk for her. "Two sugars, Cynthia?"

"Please, darling. Keeps me young."

I smiled and disappeared back to the kitchen. I had no idea what she was doing here—she rarely stopped into the actual office unless she was in the middle of buying a house, and I knew I didn't have her on the file for an appointment.

Still, I fixed her coffee and took it back out.

Mallory looked up at me with a smile. "Cynthia was just telling me that Charlotte's pregnant."

Ah, her eldest daughter.

"Congratulations!" I bent down to kiss Cynthia's cheek. "That's great news."

"It is." She beamed up at me. "Well, you know she got married recently to that nice fellow, Jonathan?"

I did. We'd both been there. "I remember."

"And now with the baby and things, they're looking for a bigger house with more of a yard because they plan on having another after this one." She brushed some hair from her eyes and took a sip of her coffee. "Jonathan's away in Vancouver on business, and Charlotte's incredibly ill with sickness, so I said I'd come in and see what you've got."

"What are they looking for?" I asked, walking around behind the desk and resting my hand on Mal's shoulder as she pulled up the listings file.

"Ideally four bedrooms, preferably a study for when Jonathan works from home, and a decent sized yard."

"Preference on bathrooms?"

"Two, but they'll go one and a half bath if the house is right."

I knew they would. Charlotte wasn't nearly as fussy as

her mother. "What's their budget?"

She gave me a ballpark number, and by the time I'd opened my mouth, Mallory already had the printer running.

For someone who'd smashed two mugs emptying the dishwasher this morning, her ability to do her job always astounded me.

"Six houses," Mal said, rolling over to the printer and almost crushing my toes in the process.

All right, so she was still rough around the edges. But it'd make a change for her to hurt me instead of herself.

As a side note, she was now banned from cleaning up any messes she'd made if the mess had sharp edges. The Band-Aid on her right hand wasn't from a paper cut.

"Now, one is a three-bed place, but I think that's only because there are two offices," she said, putting the houses down in front of Cynthia. "It's been on the market a while, but you could probably convert one back to a bedroom if you remove the shelves. Two others are four beds, and these three are five-beds, all within the price range. This one—" She pulled the bottom sheet out. "—is actually out of the budget, but only ever so slightly. We sell a lot of houses from these guys since they flip them, and they usually price a little high so they can come down."

"Ooh, I do like that one," Cynthia said. "I think they're low-balling on their budget, but these all look lovely. I'll take them to Charlotte and see what she thinks. I may have to do the first viewings if that's okay."

"Just give me a call, and I'll sort it." Mallory smiled.

Cynthia beamed at her then looked at me. "She's going to take your job if you're not careful, Cameron, darling."

I sighed and leaned against Mal's chair. "I know. I keep telling her to actually do the training, but she won't listen to me."

"I won't do it because I already know what'll happen. I'll get my license, take someone on a viewing, and trip up the stairs or something." She shook her head. "Nope. I'm happy here, half-assing it, where I can't really hurt myself."

Cynthia laughed. "That is wise, darling. Besides, the two of you make a good team."

I looked down at Mal and smiled. "We do."

"I hear you're finally moving in together."

Mal nodded. "I pretty much live there already, but I still have some stuff at my parents' house. I'm getting the rest of it this weekend."

It was a tough spot for her. Just as she'd saved enough money to get out of her parents and get an apartment, I'd told her it was ridiculous, and she should just move in with me. She'd said it was too early, but just as she was coming around to the idea, her Grandpa had a stroke.

He and Grace were still living with their parents, and when her grandfather was really ill, Mallory had come to the decision that she couldn't leave and let her mom take all the responsibility for caring for him.

Slowly, over the past six months, she'd spent more and more time at my place, effectively splitting her time between the two houses. Her stuff was in disarray—and so was my bathroom, thanks to her fucking hair products and girly shit.

Now, her grandpa was better and as ornery as ever, and she finally felt like she could leave.

It'd been a long and frustrating process for us all, but none other than her. There'd been a point where we'd all thought we'd lose him, but he was too damn stubborn to go. That hadn't meant that the decision to move out had been easy for her.

She'd gone from running out of the place to insisting on staying.

I think she was finally ready, and I was prepared to buy some storage for all the fruity-smelling body washes that were in my shower.

"I'm very happy for you," Cynthia said, tucking the property sheets into her purse. "You'll have to have a little housewarming to celebrate, darlings."

"I'll keep that in mind, Cynthia." I smiled as she finished her coffee and stood, gathering her hat and her gloves. "You let us know as soon as you're ready to take a look at some houses. We can probably get Charlotte in on a video call so she can be there, too."

"Sounds wonderful!" She kissed us both on the cheek and left.

I slumped against the desk. "She's exhausting," I said quietly.

"She means well." Mal propped her chin up on her hand and gazed up at me. "Are you sure you're ready for me to move in?"

"Hurricane, I've been trying to get you to move in for a year." I pushed hair from her eyes. "I understand why you couldn't, but yes, I'm ready. Besides, you've got more things at my house than I do."

"It's not that bad!"

"It took me five minutes to find my toothbrush this morning."

"It's not my fault you never put it back in the pot." Her red lips tugged up.

"I can't find the pot. It's surrounded by make-up and sprays that I don't even know the function of."

"The pot is on the damn wall. And you say *I'm* the dramatic one."

"You are the dramatic one." I tapped her on the nose. "You got one small cut from the broken mug this morning and declared that you were bleeding out."

"How else was I supposed to get your attention?"

"Well," I said dryly, "The giant crashing noise had already done it."

"They were still wet, and they slipped out of my hand." She sniffed. "That's why I don't do the dishwasher. Vacuuming is much safer."

"Point taken. Next time you tell me to unload the dishwasher, I'll do it. And keep you away from all other breakables in the house."

She pouted.

"All that face does is make me want to kiss you." I gently tugged on her lower lip with my thumb. "So stop it."

She didn't.

I leaned right down and kissed her, and she smiled against my lips.

God, she was adorable.

"I love you," she said softly.

I cupped her face and kissed her again. "I love you, too, Hurricane."

Thank you for reading CATASTROPHE QUEEN! I hope you enjoyed it!

Keep an eye out for sign-ups for my next romcom, THE ROOMMATE AGREEMENT, releasing March 26th. Read on for the blurb and mark your calendars!

THE ROOMMATE AGREEMENT

*Let your homeless best friend stay with you, he said. Being
roommates will be fun, he said. It's only temporary, he said.
He never said I'd fall for him.*

You know what isn't 'temporary?' The endless stream of
dirty socks in my bathroom and empty food packets under
the sofa—and don't even get me started on the hot guys
who take over my living room every Sunday to watch
sports.

I can't take anymore.

So I propose a roommate agreement. One that will bring
peace and order back to my life, complete with rules that
might just stop my newfound crush on my best friend in
its tracks.

After all, there's only so many times you can see your best
friend naked before you start to lose your mind.

Rules. They're meant to be broken... Aren't they?